VENGEANCE IS MINE

Douglas MacKinnon

An Ian Wallace Novel

"A thriller for the Tea Party generation."
—Tony Blankley, nationally syndicated columnist

THRESHOLD EDITIONS
New York   London   Toronto   Sydney   New Delhi

Threshold Editions
A Division of Simon & Schuster, Inc.
1230 Avenue of the Americas
New York, NY 10020

First Threshold Editions hardcover edition May 2012

THRESHOLD EDITIONS and colophon are trademarks of Simon & Schuster, Inc.

For information about special discounts for bulk purchases, please contact Simon & Schuster Special Sales at 1-866-506-1949 or business@simonandschuster.com.

The Simon & Schuster Speakers Bureau can bring authors to your live event. For more information or to book an event, contact the Simon & Schuster Speakers Bureau at 1-866-248-3049 or visit our website at www.simonspeakers.com.

Designed by Renata Di Biase

Manufactured in the United States of America

10   9   8   7   6   5   4   3   2   1

ISBN 978-1-4516-4097-7
ISBN 978-1-4516-4098-4 (ebook)

For the men and women of the Central Intelligence Agency who heroically and anonymously serve overseas. Patriots and protectors all. We are in your debt.

* * *

For my uncles, Tom and Peter MacKinnon. Thanks for your periodic rescue of three kids battered by extreme dysfunction. You made a real, positive, and lasting difference.

1

Chained to a metal chair in a dark cell in the bowels of Lubyanka prison in Moscow, I turn my head to the left and watch in morbid fascination as my blood continues to spurt out of the deep stab wound just inflicted into the underside of my left wrist.

With each beat of my heart, the blood squirts toward the damp, mold-covered stone ceiling like a small crimson fountain. But, with each beat, I notice that the power of the stream is less and less. Life is leaving me, and my mind is starting to shut down from the loss of oxygen.

I lick my lips, which were torn open just seconds earlier by a closed fist, and try to focus my eyes on the scene before me. The monster is walking toward me, and he means to finish me off.

I imperceptibly nod my head with the realization. That's okay, I think. The monster can have his way. I'm tired, numb, and ready for the next world. It will be a welcome relief at this point.

The gun comes out from beneath his black greatcoat. I see the hint of a smile blossoming on his malevolent face and shift my eyes toward my bloodstained pants so that the face won't be my last memory on earth.

I feel and hear him approach as his jackbooted feet scrape slowly across the dirt-encrusted cobblestone floor.

I hear the hammer of the pistol cock and wait for the finality of the pulled trigger.

There is a tremendous boom, and my head snaps up and my eyes pop open in the usual momentary confusion.

2

I was not in a prison cell in Moscow, but on a flight headed to Boston. Almost twenty years later and the nightmare still haunted me. How much better had the bullet killed me instead.

I blinked my eyes several times to clear my mind as I took a slow look around the cabin. Time to snap back to the here and now and focus on the uncertainty of modern aerodynamics rather than a life and a hope destroyed.

As my six-foot, three-inch frame sat wedged in a narrow, gray leather seat in the last row of the JetBlue flight from Washington, D.C., to Boston, I forced my mind to think of anything but Moscow and that dread dungeon. Being a person who believes in the power of negative thinking, I instantly started to wonder if the aircraft would actually make the runway safely this time, or instead, slam into the seawall and turn me into a bag of Purina worm chow.

I don't care who you are, if you fly at all, then you're going to have these funny little thoughts cross your mind from time to time. My line of work necessitates that I fly quite often. Consequently, you will always find me sitting in the last row of any aircraft on which I have booked passage.

I have several friends who are fighter pilots with the Tactical

Air Command, and they swear that the back of the aircraft is by far the safest place to be when said aircraft decides to go into the tunneling business.

A few other of my friends maintain that it makes no difference whatsoever where you sit. They contend that when the plane clips the mountaintop you will still be burned beyond recognition, and then they will take what's left of you from the crash site in a trash can liner.

I ask them, "If that is so, why do airlines place the voice and data recorders in the tail section?" At that they usually wrinkle up their foreheads and go away.

I would not want anyone to get the wrong impression of me. I am not afraid to fly. In fact, I love to fly. One of my hobbies is flying sailplanes. I have logged more than a thousand hours in them and have yet to fall out of the sky.

The really nice thing about sailplanes is that they have no engines. They don't need them. They just glide along on the warm air currents. That, however, was not the case with the Airbus 320 I now found myself occupying. Should the two engines cut out on this baby, then I knew for a fact that it would take on the gliding characteristics of a block of cement.

As it turned out, my insistence on sitting in the last row caused me to be looked upon by the head flight attendant as something lower than vermin on the species scale. The aircraft was very sparsely populated on this late afternoon flight. In fact, I counted only ten passengers in all. I congratulated myself on being so observant. As a former government type turned private investigator, it was my business to be observant, and I seemed to be doing a passable job of it today.

I'm no Allan Pinkerton, mind you. But still pretty good. Just as I was congratulating myself on my innate counting ability, a little kid with a runny nose came out of the lavatory behind me and went to sit next to his mother. That made the count eleven passengers, not ten. Maybe being unobservant could be turned into a unique and valuable asset with my clients.

Turning my head away in shame, I noticed two very pretty blond flight attendants who were hard at work in the galley to my left. They were getting our snack trays ready so we hungry passengers would not be without peanuts, warm cookies, or soda for the next hour and ten minutes. Of course, it would take me that long just to open the bag of peanuts the airlines superglue shut as their little joke on the passengers, but nonetheless, I was always happy to get them.

I was very carefully checking these two out for clues or concealed weapons when I noticed the head flight attendant slowly making her way toward me from the front of the aircraft. She smiled down at me and said, "Today must be your lucky day, Mr. Wallace."

I looked up at her and noticed that her name tag said "Jean." I have always made it a policy of mine that if a waitress or flight attendant or car mechanic is going to be nice enough to wear a name tag, then I will be courteous enough to call them by their name. I worked my way through college as a waiter and bartender and lost count of how many times customers addressed me as "Boy" or "Hey, you." Name tags are nice.

"And why is today my lucky day, Jean?"

She was wearing a white short-sleeve shirt and under her blue apron a fairly short blue skirt that made her look most fetching to this road-weary traveler. She also had very pretty, evenly arranged white teeth that I strongly suspected came from a very good dental lab. As a former college and minor league hockey player, I knew a thing or two about good and *bad* dental work. She turned up the candlepower as she answered me.

"Because we're going to let you sit up front."

I leaned across her to peer toward the front of the long aisle where I could see the heads of a few people reading the *Washington Post* or magazines.

"You really want me to sit up there?"

As she nodded her head energetically, I noticed my face reflected perfectly in the glasses that framed her pale blue eyes.

That in turn reminded me of a problem I sometimes have. I make it a practice of trying to only wear mirrored sunglasses. The main reason is that the bad guy can never tell if you're looking at him, and besides that, I happen to think it adds to my all-around "hard-ass" look, which I'm still trying daily to perfect. They have only one real drawback that I'm aware of, and that is that they are *real* mirrors. I have actually had women friends of mine fix their makeup or comb their hair while "looking" into my eyes. A very strange feeling.

I did not want to be guilty of the same distraction, so I averted my eyes, which came to rest on her breasts. This, I thought, would not do, either, so I stared at her forehead.

"Do I have a choice, Jean?"

Ah-hah! I caught her. In the post-9/11 environment we all fly in, I think Jean was used to passengers jumping at any offer or command.

"Of course you have a choice, Mr. Wallace. Don't you want to sit up front? It's much more comfortable than back here near the galley and restrooms."

The two flight attendants in the galley had now stopped

what they were doing to listen in on the conversation. They were obviously as stunned as Jean to hear that a passenger might decline to move. I don't think I could have had anymore of their attention had I told them that in my spare time, I like to experiment with explosive radios and underwear.

"Well, Jean, it's not that I don't want to sit up front as much as it is that I like it fine right here."

Jean ran her fingers through her red hair as she started to get a little nervous. I would not have put it past her to have the captain return to Dulles Airport outside Washington, D.C., and have me forcibly removed from the aircraft until they could check my name against the totally useless "no-fly" list.

"Pardon me. But that makes no sense," she said softly, with just a slight tremble in her voice.

Out of the corner of my eye, I could have sworn that I saw the shorter of the two flight attendants quietly reaching for the heavy metal coffeepot.

"Well, it's like this, Jean. Normally, the more well-to-do people tend to sit up front. I know you don't have a first class and all on this airline, but let's face it, old habits are hard to break. What if I go up there and slurp my coffee or something. Maybe I'll offend Tad or Muffy."

I thought I was being clever and witty but that was obviously not the consensus among the three flight attendants. The only reaction I got out of them was three worried little smiles. They were still not quite sure that I was not going to snap and run toward the flight deck or start working the lever on the exit door.

Jean was nothing if not persistent. "Are you sure, sir? You see, the plane is very light this flight, and the captain would like to balance the load."

I smiled back up at her. "Thanks but no thanks, Jean. I always fly in the last row. I like it back here."

The three of them exchanged a knowing look. He's not a terrorist or a nut, they were thinking. No, he's worse than that. He's a coward.

Jean looked down at me as if I had gotten out of bed one too many times headfirst. "I think I understand, sir."

As she was walking back up the aisle to select her next victim, I wanted to say, "But Jean, you don't understand: I love to fly. I'm not the sniveling little weasel you now think I am."

Pride, however, told me that discretion was the better part of valor, and for once I listened.

3

I did not have any luggage to pick up. I never have any luggage to pick up. In the past I have made the mistake of having an airline tag my bags and take them away on that little conveyor belt. Fool me once, shame on you. Fool me twice, and I'm getting a measly little check in the mail from my airline's insurance company.

Once, on a trip from Boston to Chicago, one of my bags ended up in London, England. As in the land of tea, crumpets, and the kick-ass Premier League. Needless to say, I never got it back. The last I heard, my bag had been blown up in a controlled explosion by MI5.

That said, I'd still rather take my chances trying to retrieve my luggage from some James Bond "Q" wannabe at MI5 than have to endure one more pat-down from a rotund TSA troll who never met a doughnut—or a breast—he didn't drool over. But, as I *really* didn't want to get radiated in their still undertested full-body-scan machines from a clearly inept future, I always opted for the full-body *massage* from a TSA sloth. Unfortunately—but not surprisingly—the guy who inspected me on the way out of D.C. seemed to enjoy keeping his paws near my nether region for an awkwardly long time.

Seriously, if I were the emperor of the United States for just one day, one of the first things I'd do would be to disband the TSA and turn the entire operation over to the private sector. In the parade of our government being intrusive and out of control, the beyond-incompetent TSA is carrying the baton and wearing the shiniest jackboots of the lot.

I walked outside the terminal at Logan Airport and thought, It's great to be back in Boston. It was five-thirty in the afternoon and a very balmy 75 degrees. I have always loved Washington, D.C., but if you happen to be one of the unfortunates in that town who live without central air-conditioning in the summer, then you don't breathe the air, you walk into it. Heavy does not begin to describe it as its humid weight settles in upon your shoulders for the day.

Aside from the change in humidity, I missed Boston itself. I had been down in D.C. for two months on a protection assignment, so I was just glad to be back in town. My town.

The gentleman I had to protect down there was a former sleazy trial lawyer who was now the head of a very liberal think tank called "Equal Justice for Illegals," which he had created in response to the continuing unlawful border crossings taking place across the U.S.–Mexican frontier. This guy was in favor of many things, but the protection of our sovereign borders was not one of them. Aside from actively trying to smuggle illegal aliens into our nation, he also dabbled in the fight to legalize dangerous narcotics and to abolish the Second Amendment. A true man of the people.

Because of his exuberant and public flaunting of his abuse of the rule of law, he had received several death threats in the last few months. I'm sure more than a few good old boys as well as a number of my buddies from "Southie" had this creep on their "send a *form letter* death threat" mailing list.

That said, he was an extremely wealthy socialist—aren't they all—and times were still tough for working stiffs like me. I needed some money, and he needed protection. So I took the gig.

Because of the death threats, he was willing to pay any price to protect his "flag-burning, America last, the military is for losers" ass and way of thinking. As I had come recommended to him by a former "associate" of mine in the D.C. area, I knew he wanted to close the deal instantly and get me down to his estate. Knowing that, and because his politics and way of life turned my stomach, I pinged him for six thousand dollars a week, plus expenses, for the protection assignment. Of course, only after I left did I find out that this former sleazy trial lawyer turned liberal activist had been prepared to pay twice that amount and thought he got me on the cheap.

All in all, it was a very boring job. Someone did place a pipe bomb in his mailbox one night, but nothing came of it, except for a new mailbox and a visit from some folks from the Department of Homeland Security.

"Mr. Equal Justice for Illegals" lived in McLean, Virginia, a very exclusive suburb of Washington. And the one thing this guy did manage to accomplish was to regularly attract protesters who marched in front of his home and through his very upper-yuppie neighborhood.

For that very reason, I strongly suspect that the McLean town council placed the bomb in his mailbox. I think they felt that a town house in Georgetown would be more to his and their liking.

I finally told him that he would be much better off hiring a local security firm for his protection. My thinking being that this would save him some money, and get me out of D.C. and back to the Red Sox and their current ten-game losing streak.

Much to my surprise, he agreed all too readily. The reason, I fear, had nothing to do with money and everything to do with his very attractive twenty-four-year-old daughter, Tiffany.

Tiffany had somehow decided that I was just the "conservative dirtbag" to use and abuse to get even with her totalitarian father. While sensuously framed in six-inch black stilettos, a short black leather skirt, and some kind of see-through dark blue DKNY blouse that did its job by highlighting her overflowing black bra, she decided to implement her plan and test her acting skills all in the course of one night while the three of us were having dinner at P.J. Clarke's in D.C. After having knocked back a few too many white Russians, she looked at me with a leer and said in a very loud but cute southern voice, "Ian, may I come back to your room again tonight, so you can teach me some more gymnastics?"

At that point her father started to choke to death on his perfectly prepared veggie burger while the three twenty-something women at the table next to ours instantly uploaded text and photos of the choking onto their Facebook accounts.

I had never even touched his daughter, but that defense had long since sailed away along with Tiffany's virginity. The next day he gave me a check for services rendered. It's not that I didn't trust the man, but before I went to the airport, I went to his bank and had the check certified.

4

Since I'm Scottish by heritage and have been known to pinch a penny in my day, I thought I would take the subway back to my office rather than a cab. To get to the T station from Logan Airport, you catch the Massport shuttle bus. They used to charge you for the ride, but now it's free. Another wonderful service provided to its citizens by the great state of Massachusetts. Little wonder that every time I cross in over the commonwealth's borders I feel like I am entering the former Soviet Union. Creeping socialism, Bay State–style.

As a conservative who believes in limited government and lower taxes, it's always a bitter pill to swallow, but home is still home. Plus, there has been a glimmer of hope of late as the good citizens of Massachusetts finally seem to be turning away from one-party rule and the lies of the nanny state.

No matter, it still felt great to be back in Boston. One ride on the T, however, made me want to go screaming back to D.C. as fast as humanly possible.

I paid my fare at the airport T station for the Blue Line and proceeded to walk downstairs to the platform to wait for my train. So what's the first thing I saw when I got down there? A street person taking a whiz against the wall. He was pissing on what looked like a mural of a 747, and again, to my trained eyes, it looked as if he hadn't missed one inch of the aircraft. Delta should hire this guy to de-ice their aircraft during the long, cold Boston winters.

"Hey, you!" I yelled. Unobservant *with* a limited vocabulary. No wonder my bank account was empty.

He looked over his shoulder at me and smiled a toothless grin. Not only was he taking a squirt in public, but he was also singing the Harvard fight song. He seemed to know all the words, which only confirmed to me that you are destined for failure once you graduate from that glorified trade school.

My very old red-and-white train finally wheezed and coughed its way into the station. I only had to take it to State Street station. Just three stops away. Do you think I could go three lousy stops without witnessing a freak show? No such luck.

No sooner did we pull away than an extremely well-built Hispanic girl began screaming in Spanish and pulled a knife on her seat companion. I had just started to admire her thighs, which were covered in jeans that looked like she had used a spray gun to put on, when I caught the flash of blue steel in the late afternoon sunshine. "Blue steel." That's detective talk. I think it's somewhere in the handbook I have along with my badge, whistle, and plastic handcuffs.

She screamed nonstop at this guy as her long black hair flew around her head. It seemed to bother him not at all. He sat there wearing a filthy NEA cap and rose-colored sunglasses. He was about fifty years old and did not seem to fear for his safety.

Possibly, I thought, this gentleman was a former head of a corrupt teachers' union who put his perks and benefits well before the needs of the schoolchildren of Boston. If that was the case, then Lord knows he had it coming. I got to State Street in one piece and bid the Puerto Rican Bundys a fond farewell.

My office is on Park Street across the street from Boston Common. The city looked great as I walked a few blocks down Washington Street, then cut up Winter Street, and presto, hit Park Street and reached my office building.

The office itself is in a great location. Aside from the beautiful view of the common, if I ever get a burning desire to go to the zoo, well then, the State House is just up the hill on my right. I can go and watch the state reps fighting each other for graft, free tickets, and the chance to kiss the governor's ass. You are always permitted to look at them in their cages, but you're never allowed to feed them. On more than one occasion, they have been known to bite their constituents. Usually anytime the constituent has the nerve to ask the state rep what they actually do to earn their salary.

I walked into the rather ostentatious lobby of my building and was greeted by the sight of our "security guard." At the very least, he must have been a veteran of the Spanish-American War. He may have been strong, tough, and capable during his heyday, but as of now, if a ticked-off Camp Fire Girl wanted access to the building, Father Time was not about to keep her out.

He got up from his desk as I entered the lobby. With Frank, you never know. He might decide to draw down on you.

"Ease up, Frank. It's only me."

He smiled at me as he sat back down. Even though he had most likely once dated Methuselah's grandmother, he still somehow retained all of his very thick white hair, which he parted in the middle. Below that were two big brown eyes, which were magnified tenfold by the Coke bottle glasses he wore. Every time he blinked, it looked like they were lowering the curtain at Radio City Music Hall.

He waved me over to his desk.

"Mr. Wallace, it's great to see you back in town. When did you get in?"

I sat on the edge of his highly polished wooden desk. "Frank, look, how many times do I have to tell you? Don't call me Mr. Wallace. Call me Ian. I hate when you call me Mr. Wallace. Anybody your age should not have to call anyone 'mister.' Just call me Ian, okay?"

Frank grinned at me with his tobacco-stained false teeth. The man smoked like a chimney and was the sworn enemy of all things politically correct. Aside from his dislike of the PC crowd, the only things keeping him alive were booze, tobacco, and Slim Jims. The three building blocks of life on the planet Flatulence.

"Anything you say, Mr. Wallace."

Why do I waste my time? "Frank . . . never mind. It's good to see you, too, buddy."

I reached into the paper bag I was carrying. "Oh, here, before I forget. I brought you a present."

I laid the current issue of *Playboy* magazine on his desk. Yes, Frank was also a dirty old man. As of last count, he had been married four times and had fourteen children. Miss June might even cause Frank to experience a few palpitations. He was quietly humming to himself and flipping to the centerfold as I caught the elevator to the third floor.

I have to admit, this building was really very nice. If anything, it was too nice. More-than-I-could-afford nice. Still, it did impress the clients, and money wasn't everything.

A friend of mine who headed up the most successful

lobbying shop in Washington said it was always a mistake to try to save money on a cheap office in a bad location.

"Ian," he drawled in his very thick Mississippi accent, "I haven't met the client yet who walked into a shithole of an office and said, 'Damn! I want to give my money and business to this sumbitch!' They want to see flash before they give you the cash. Now pass me that bottle of Scotch."

The elevator opened to a cream-colored hallway with very plush royal blue carpeting. Drop your car keys down in that stuff, and it's time to get out the metal detector.

My office was off to the left of the elevators. It was behind a very heavy oak door with raised gold lettering that said WALLACE INVESTIGATIONS. I was going to use "Federal Bureau of Investigation" or "Interpol," but they were both taken.

The one distinguishing feature on my door, and which I was quite proud of, was the seal of the province of Nova Scotia, just below WALLACE INVESTIGATIONS. Seeing as how my family had emigrated from Scotland to Nova Scotia—New Scotland, for those who are not in the know—and then down to Boston in the guise of my paternal grandfather, I thought the seal of Nova Scotia, which consists of the Scottish flag, or the Cross of St. Andrew, with a red lion rampant on a yellow shield directly in the middle, would cover most of my family bases. A real attention getter, and to this day it's the best seal I've ever seen.

Looking down from the seal, I took out my keys, opened the lock, and went inside. Mrs. Casey, who happens to be my assistant and keeper, was long gone. Five o'clock comes and she is streaking for the elevator. A NASCAR driver should be so lucky to draft behind her at Daytona.

After being gone for two months, the office seemed a

little smaller than when I last saw it. But neat. Very neat. Mrs. Casey did not like dirt. She was forever cleaning up after me. Thought I was a pig. I would not argue the point. But to Mrs. Casey, a pig should only be seen in a pen or at the buffet at IHOP. Not in her office signing her paycheck.

Wallace Investigations consisted of a small reception area where the stern Mrs. Casey sat, a fair-sized conference room with a table for six, and my office, which was located about five feet behind Mrs. Casey's desk.

All in all, I had a little more than four hundred square feet of office space. In Dallas, Washington, or Miami, four hundred square feet might rent for a very reasonable price. In the heart of Boston, however, you not only had to sign over your first-born child to the leasing company, but also have your mother on call in case the CEO was "frisky." A whole new category of outrageously expensive.

Fortunately for me, I was subleasing from a former client who was now in the state prison for the next seven or so years. He used to be a very well-respected lawyer in Beantown, until he decided to siphon off ten million from the account of a fe-male billionaire he was sleeping with at the time.

To hear him tell it, she wasn't even that pissed-off about the money. It was more when she came home early and found him bonking the maid. Once confronted with that, she went out and hired an even more well-known "flesh-eating" lawyer and pressed full charges.

Not only did this guy let me sublease at a rate that would at least spare my mom from the oldest profession, but he let me use his very upscale furniture as well. In return, all he wanted from me was to remind some of the tougher guys in the slam to make sure no one in the joint decided his new name should be Nancy. A fair and equitable trade-off.

The walls of my reception area were painted a soft eggshell white. A fairly thick beige carpet covered the floor and highlighted Mrs. Casey's elegant desk. A small emerald-green leather sofa and two Queen Anne chairs surrounded a glass-topped coffee table. All in all, quite nice.

I picked up the mail from Mrs. Casey's desk and opened the door to my private office. Then I dropped all of the mail onto the floor. Not because there was anything wrong with my motor functions, but because there was a gun barrel pressed against my temple. The metal was very cold and hard against my skin.

5

Attached to the gun was a very deep voice.

"Where the hell did they dig up that relic downstairs?"

I started to breathe again.

"Holy shit, Phil. One of these days you're going to pull that act once too often and get your head blown off."

Phil laughed and put his Glock back in its shoulder holster. A weapon he technically wasn't allowed to have in the United States, but liked to carry for self-protection and as a way to say "screw you" to liberal politicians.

I shook his extended hand warmly and directed him to a seat in front of my desk. Phil was Philip Andrews, a twenty-year veteran of the Central Intelligence Agency and one of the best friends a person could ever have. Except for his fixation with practical jokes, he was a good man to know. The very fact that he was a smart-ass was what was keeping him from the big time at the Agency.

The CIA was funny like that. What they would reward you for in the field was looked down upon once you were back in the States. Sure, be original out there where your ass might be on the line, but you had better be prim and proper once you were back inside the walls at Langley.

It was one of the reasons I got out. I gave six years of my life to that organization and never felt at peace with myself. It was never that I felt the job I was being asked to perform was unimportant in the scheme of things, because it most certainly was. Rather, it was because I was starting to enjoy my work too much. I was scared of what I was becoming. Of what they were turning me into. I did my part. I wanted out. I wanted some semblance of a normal life. Whatever that might mean.

Phil just sat there across from me with a stupid grin on his face.

"Are you going to say anything," I asked, "or just sit there like the village idiot wannabe we both know you to be?"

He leaned back in the chair and put his feet up on my desk.

"Yeah, I'm going to say something. Why didn't you get in touch with me while you were down in D.C.? Last I heard, we were still friends."

I reached over and knocked his feet off my desk.

"First of all, keep your filthy feet off the rented furniture. Second, I did try to get in touch with you. I called your house, and Karen told me you were out of the country."

He smiled again. Phil felt that since he paid eight thousand dollars to get his teeth capped, he was going to get his money's worth. The fact that U.S. taxpayers got stuck with the bill made no difference to him. Phil was now smiling for all of America.

"A minor technicality, Wallace. I got back in last week."

My nerves were now a little on edge. Phil never called me Wallace unless there was something not so pleasant coming right behind it. I got up from my desk and went over to my little refrigerator. "You want a Pepsi?"

"I'll take a beer if you've got one."

I shook my head. "No can do. It's Pepsi or the water cooler out in the hall."

Phil laughed. "I forgot I was dealing with Mr. Clean. Yeah, give me a Pepsi."

I threw him one and sat back down.

"All right, Phil, let's have it. What's the bad news?"

Phil opened the Pepsi, which sprayed all over his gray pin-striped suit. "Ah shit, Ian."

I went out to Mrs. Casey's desk and snagged a bunch of pop-up Kleenex from her blue decorator box. I came back in and handed them to Phil, then watched as he wiped the Pepsi off of his suit.

"You know," I said, "that tissue is leaving tiny white flecks all over your suit."

Phil looked down at his chest.

"Ah shit, Ian."

He proceeded to brush them off his suit as if they were baby scorpions. I thought he was going to beat himself to death.

"Phil, if you're about done there, can we get on with this?"

He was still picking at his suit as he answered me.

"We have some work for you."

I laughed at nothing. "By 'we,' I assume you mean the Agency."

Phil was no longer smiling. "It's important, Ian."

God, it's funny. You think that you'll be different. That they will leave you in peace. That you won't become a cliché. Let you walk away and forget you ever heard of the CIA. But you never really believe it. You're always waiting for the phone call or the tap on the shoulder. It's like organized crime. You can walk away, but you're never totally out. Never.

"Look, Phil, I left the Agency for some very important

reasons. You know why. If I wanted to do their work, I'd still be in. I'm out now, and I'm still alive. Let's just leave it that way, okay?"

Phil got up from his chair and went over to the window. I didn't have to get up to know what he was looking at. I had it memorized. He was staring at hundreds of Bostonians streaming down through the doors of the Park Street subway station on their way home from another tough day of just trying to get by in the world.

The only ones who still had it easy in this country were the hedge fund managers you hear so much about on the news. Well, at least the ones not in prison or being blamed by the liberal leadership in Congress for every disaster including the fictional and budget-busting "Global Warming, aka Climate Change."

Phil turned to face me.

"Ian, I'm your friend. . . ."

"Yeah, I know. That's why they sent you. To take advantage of you, *and* our friendship."

Phil leaned his lanky six-foot body against the window frame. "Yeah, that's true. But you can just as easily say no to me as to anyone else."

I focused my gaze on the blue sky visible over his left shoulder instead of on his penetrating dark eyes. "They think it will be harder for me because of you."

Phil smirked. "Maybe they're right."

"They're wrong, Phil. And you're wrong if you think the way they do. The answer is no."

Phil walked back over to my desk, sat down, and leaned across a fake mahogany desk clock I got with a bottle of cologne.

"You're saying no and you don't even know what the deal is yet."

I took off my gold collar bar, loosened my tie, and undid my collar button.

"That's right, buddy. And I don't want to know. I'm out."

Phil's tanned face was starting to get red with anger.

"What's that, your stock answer now? 'I'm out. I'm out.' Well, it's not that simple, Ian. It doesn't work that way. You can't just stop the world and say you want to get off. You can't stick your head in the sand and wait for the trouble to pass you by, because it won't. It will bite you right in your ass. We live in a real world and as current events keep demonstrating, it's getting worse all the time."

Phil knew things about me. He knew lots of things about me. As one of my best friends, he knew the good things about me. As a former colleague with the Agency, he also knew the bad things about me. The very bad things.

Things that I did not want to be reminded about today or ever. Things that I had somewhat successfully suppressed the last few years.

Phil really was a close friend, but just having him standing before me was opening my mind's eye to terrible things. To horrific memories. To a pain that had all but consumed me years earlier.

I was very happy to see my old friend, but I needed him to leave soon lest he tear open the scabs I still carried.

I raised my hand to speak but he went on before I could say anything.

"I know what you're going to say. That you paid your dues ten times over. That you owe this country nothing, and it owes you everything. Don't you think I know that? Don't you think

I feel that way? I understand why you left. But it's the same reason I stay in. The pressure just pushed us in opposite directions. We both have a responsibility, Ian. For the rest of our lives we will have that responsibility."

Pressure had nothing to do with me leaving the Agency, as Phil well knew. I closed my eyes and gently rubbed my forehead as he continued.

"Don't you think I look at some of these clowns in their thousand-dollar suits carrying their four-hundred-dollar briefcases and think, Gee, wouldn't it be nice to be the director of security for some Fortune 500 company for the rest of my life. Don't you think I would like to be a full-time husband and a full-time father? Don't you think that there are times when I just want to walk away from it? Cash it in and be 'Average Joe'?"

He was baiting me to ask the obvious question, so I bit.

"So why don't you? Go corporate security and make a ton of money. It'd make Karen and the kids a whole lot happier."

He gave me his sincere look. And with Phil, that's just what it was. Sincere.

"Because I can't, Ian. I believe in what I'm doing. I believe in the Agency. I believe this country is better off because of what we do. Because of you and me. It's that simple. Everything changed when New York and D.C. got hit, and I just can't walk away from that responsibility like . . ."

Phil realized he had crossed a line that both of us knew should never be crossed and stopped himself in mid-sentence. He knew why I left, and it had nothing to do with any psychobabble bullshit. It had everything to do with a mind-searing pain that destroyed my life. "Like me, Phil? Well screw that!" I yelled. "Where do you get off preaching to me like I'm some goddamn five-year-old in Sunday school? I put in my time. I went straight to the ninth circle of hell for this country, and for the Agency. And do you know what I have to show for it?"

He nodded his head yes, but I told him anyway.

"Damn right you know. I've got a lifetime supply of nightmares, buddy. I still wake up some nights drenched in a cold sweat. And do you know what's worst of all? I wake up alone. No wife. No children. Zip. So don't you ever friggin' tell me what my responsibility to this nation is. You've got an Agency problem, pal. Use Agency people to solve it."

I could actually feel my heart pounding in my chest as my mind took me back to Moscow, to both the highest and lowest points of my life.

"We can't, Ian. It's domestic. Even with all that's gone on lately with terrorism, Congress is still after our butts. They just don't trust us. They still blame us for Iraq. We don't need to be in violation of our charter."

That was certainly true enough. You had to wonder sometimes if the members of Congress worked for the American people or for those who would like to dismantle the CIA one spy at a time. Not even the ongoing efforts to stop terrorist attacks against the United States could make some of those people believe in the need for the CIA and human intelligence on the ground.

Partisan politics on both sides of the aisle fostered an environment where it was much easier to blame the CIA for the growing shortcomings of Congress. While most congressmen, intellectually at least, agreed that the post-9/11 United States would be forever more a target of fanatical Muslim terrorists, they were not going to let that nightmarish fact prevent them from doing or saying anything necessary to get reelected. Ignoring the warnings they got from the CIA in closed-door briefings, and then announcing to the media that they never got such a briefing when the shit hit the fan, was just par for the course in Washington.

I ran my hand across my forehead and up through my still thick black hair. I was not surprised to find it was wet with sweat. "Well, get the FBI. We've both got friends over there and that's what they're for."

"It's not like that, Ian. No need for the Bureau to know anything about this. It's just a simple protection job."

Why did simple suddenly sound like a four-letter word?

Phil relaxed a little and took a sip of his Pepsi. As he put it back down, I noticed the can had left a ring on my desk.

I tried to slow my heartbeat and lighten the mood. Without meaning to, Phil was pushing me to the edge.

"Mrs. Casey is not going to be happy about that," I said, pointing to the ring.

He picked up the can and wiped off my desk with his elbow. This was the same guy who was worried about a little Pepsi on his suit earlier. Phil got back to the game plan.

"The Agency will pay you forty grand to be this guy's shadow for two weeks. And don't tell me you can't use the money, bub. That is at least five times what you'd normally get for two weeks' worth of work."

I gave him my shocked expression.

"Whatever do you mean? I won the Megabucks lottery last year. I just do this for a hobby now."

Not even a grin. He just sat there and stared at me. Looking stoic.

"Ian, this is honestly important to the country. No bullshit. This is big-time."

I listened to the sounds of the traffic outside my window.

It's strange how background noise can be perceived as silence by most of us. Is there any such thing as true silence, I wondered? I don't think so. Even in a 100 percent soundproof room, you would still hear the sounds of your own body. Your heart, your breathing, your motion. Right now, I wished I was in a soundproof room so I wouldn't have to listen to Phil.

"I know it's important, Phil. I believe you. I know you wouldn't be here if you felt otherwise. But the answer is still no. Get someone else."

Phil had no intention of getting anyone else. He was stubborn like that.

"All right, Ian, I'm not supposed to tell you this, but as a friend I feel I owe it to you."

I tried to look bored with the conversation. I had no interest in this case no matter what I was about to hear. Or so I thought.

"The guy you have to babysit," said Phil, "is an Ivan. The people we want you to protect him from are the Russian Mafia. Contrary to popular belief, they really do represent, as the saying goes, *a clear and present danger* to our country."

That news definitely piqued my curiosity but still I said nothing.

"Ian, what I'm about to tell you is highly classified. It could put my ass in a sling if anyone finds out I told you."

I shrugged. "So don't tell me."

Phil scratched his head and moved some of his thinning blond hair. "I wish it were that easy, Ian. I feel like shit telling you, but you have a right to know."

He was honestly torn by what he was telling me. He was one of the most decent people I had ever known. His sense of honor and duty had been at times all-consuming.

"I don't want to know anymore."

"You want to know this."

"All right, you win. What!?"

Pain seemed to flash in Phil's eyes before he spoke. Not his own, I realized, but pain he was feeling for me.

"Our intel folks tell us Vladimir Ivanchenko is headed to Boston."

6

The line was not only crossed, but obliterated. With that one sentence Phil had pushed my mind so far over the edge that inside I was falling out of control toward a blackness of pure, inescapable evil.

It felt as if a bomb had just exploded inside my head. All I could see was red. Hate. Pure hate filled my mind. Phil was still talking but I could not understand what he was saying.

I was aware of tears filling my eyes and overflowing onto my cheeks. I could not control them. I could not control myself. I could actually feel myself losing it. Completing the circuit from sane to insanity. Crazy with fury that had lain dormant in me for many years. Fury that had no outlet until now. Until this very moment. I focused once again on Phil.

"I'll take the fuckin' assignment," I hissed.

Phil shook his head. "Ian, this can't be a vendetta against Ivanchenko. It has to be done right."

I jumped up and swept the pictures of my nephew, Christopher, and niece, Julie, right off my desk. They hit the wall and their glass fronts shattered like the many lives Ivanchenko had destroyed over the years.

"What the hell!" I screamed. "Are you deaf!? I said I'll take the goddamned case. Who am I protecting?"

Phil left his chair, went over to the wall, and picked up the pictures off the floor. He brushed the glass from the young smiling faces and put them back on my desk.

I looked at their pictures and cried. I just sat there and cried. I cried for the unborn child I would never know. I cried for the woman I had loved. But most of all, I simply cried for myself. For my loneliness.

As tears and mucus dripped from my bowed head onto my suit, shirt, and tie, I felt Phil walk up beside me, pat my shoulder, and press some tissues into my right hand.

After a few minutes I stood and walked out of my office and into the men's room out in the hall. I spent five minutes washing my face, cleaning my clothes, and trying to get my breathing back under control. When I came back into the office, Phil had cleaned up most of the glass.

"Thank you." I smiled weakly. "I'm okay now."

Phil squinted at me. "That's bullshit, buddy. But you'll be okay someday. Not now. Not a few months from now. But soon. If anyone deserves it, it's you. I'm just so sorry I caused all of this."

I walked over to Phil and patted him on the arm. "You didn't cause any of this," I said in a deep whisper. "We both know who did, and you just told me where to find him."

"Ian. *Don't.* Don't do anything stupid. Life is full of shitstorms, and you've been under more than your fair share. Last time I checked, you were a Christian and deep believer so don't make things worse by not thinking."

Phil was my friend, and he was concerned. He felt for me, but he didn't feel my pain. He couldn't. And I was glad. No one should ever experience such pain. Such torture. Such loneliness.

Well, no, I thought. I was wrong. One person should experience such pain. He should experience it slowly. Glacier slow. Knowing full well the only escape for him would be the finality of death. The sooner the better. But not too soon. His debts were many, and they were now mine to collect.

There is a famous old Scottish expression, *Revenge is a dish best served cold.* I agree completely. I believe in revenge. I believe in an eye for an eye. I have always thought that those who turned the other cheek were wrong. Many times, dead wrong. I don't forgive and I don't forget.

I remember you, Vladimir, I thought to myself. I remember everything. Things are different now, however. This is Boston, not Moscow. You're coming to my city now and will have to play by my rules.

Phil was reading my mind. "Ian, they're dead. And dead is dead. Nothing you do now will ever bring them back."

I took a deep breath and let it out slowly.

"I know. Dead is dead"—I turned to look out the window at the darkening blue sky—"is dead." I then lowered my head, stared down at the floor, and whispered, *"The Lord does indeed help those who help themselves. Maybe I'll be His instrument on this one."*

Phil narrowed his eyes at my whispered ravings and then pulled an envelope out of his coat pocket. "What . . . never mind. Forget it. I told you. I did my job. I'm not your babysitter. You're gonna do what you want anyway, so sit down and let me tell you what's what."

For the next half hour he told me about it. The guy I had to protect was a pre-Glasnost Soviet defector by the name of

Georgy Barkagan. He was now a full professor at the Massachusetts Institute of Technology. His specialty was computer software. The word was that he was a true genius in his field. His project for the last year had been running software for the Pentagon for their still unacknowledged lasers in space program.

That was always the hitch with those programs. Getting the software to work. The hardware was a piece of cake to the boys and girls at the Lawrence Livermore Lab in California. Give us the software, they said, and we will give you the world.

It appeared that was just what Dr. Barkagan was about to do. He was that close to perfecting the software. Good news for the United States government and even better news for Barkagan. One of the deals he made with his CIA and FBI handlers was that anything else he came up with in terms of "nonmilitary" technology was his. He would own it, and the U.S. government would help him overcome any pesky patent problems.

Soon after perfecting the laser software, Barkagan came up with a more profitable software. He created an anti-spam and anti-spying software that soon became mandatory for almost every home and business computer in the nation. To date, Barkagan had pocketed north of $300 million from his "exclusive, noncompete" software programs.

Several highly respected computer and software firms had complained bitterly to anyone in the government who would listen that *they* had already created such software but were being blocked at every opportunity to market it.

Mysteriously, they stopped complaining after visits from extremely tough-looking federal agents who came bearing a generous checkbook and a very strict confidentiality agreement.

Barkagan's phenomenal success did not go unnoticed. *Forbes, Fortune,* the *Wall Street Journal,* and several business blogs had done articles on the former Soviet defector who was "well on his way to billionaire status."

These publications and outlets had a wide, respected, influential, and diverse readership. Among their most loyal readers were a group of men who resided in the "Little Odessa" section of New York City.

Most who met these gentlemen would describe them as "hardworking, somewhat hard-edged immigrants."

That would be one description. The Federal Bureau of Investigation had another name for them—the Russian Mafia.

With the fall of the former Soviet Union, the spies, thugs, and killers formerly employed by the KGB suddenly found themselves out of work. Being a creative lot, they soon figured out that their considerable, if dark, talents could be put to use in the always promising fields of drug dealing, arms dealing, protection, blackmail, extortion, money laundering, stock manipulation, and the ever popular murder.

Like any good corporation, once they met with unrivaled success in the former Soviet Union they decided to open branch offices around the world. By far their most successful office outside of Moscow was their Little Odessa branch in the New York City borough of Brooklyn.

U.S. law enforcement officials had established a clear relationship between the Russian Mafia and La Cosa Nostra, the Italian-American criminal network in the United States. Phil surprised me a bit by saying the LCN was cooperating with the Russian Mafia on activities related to gambling, extortion, prostitution, and fraud.

Cooperative efforts between the Russian Mafia and the

Colombian drug cartels were also well documented and were centered in Miami, where the local FBI office characterized the Russian gangsters as "very brutal . . . they are very sophisticated. They are computer literate. They hit the ground running."

They picked Miami because it represents a gateway to both the United States and Latin America. The Russian Mafia is so inventive and well capitalized that the Drug Enforcement Administration and FBI disrupted one scheme that involved a plan to use a Russian-built submarine to smuggle cocaine from Colombia to the United States.

The Russian Mafia is also known or is reported to be involved in criminal activity with other major international organized crime groups, including the Sicilian Mafia, the 'Ndrangheta, the Camorra, the Boryokudan (Japanese Yakuza), Chinese Triads, Korean criminal groups, Turkish drug traffickers, Hamas, Hezbollah, Colombian drug cartels, and other South American drug organizations. These groups have cooperated with their Russian counterparts in international narcotics trafficking, money laundering, counterfeiting, and various other terrorist activities.

Phil took a break from his well-prepared lecture, had a sip of his Pepsi, and looked up at me.

"Are you getting sick of this, 'cause I can stop."

I shook my head. "No, the background may be helpful. It's Jake with me."

"It's what?" Phil asked, suddenly distracted.

"Jake. As in good. As in continue."

"You've really got to stop watching all those forties movies on AMC," he said, shaking his head, before continuing the background.

The Russian Mafia took full notice of their former countryman and his well-publicized success in the United States. They felt the same sort of pride in him that a starving wolf would find in a sheep who had gorged itself on feed for years, was now fat beyond belief, and was unable to move from the middle of a very lonely and deserted field.

The Russian Mafia, like the wolf, felt it was its duty to put the sheep out of its bloated misery. "Why else," they often asked themselves, "would the sheep purposefully become so fat, if not to help others less fortunate?"

With that altruistic thought in mind, the Russian immigrants in Little Odessa picked up the phone, dialed Moscow, and summoned a particularly twisted individual to deal with Dr. Barkagan and his newfound wealth.

Phil finished telling me his amusing Russian fable and then answered the few questions I had.

While Phil thought—and in fact, knew—he had me cornered on this one, I also knew that his ass was in a sling and I could make certain reasonable demands. As in now.

"Sounds like I'm going to need some help on this one."

Phil absentmindedly nodded his head like someone was telling him the sun rises in the east or that Lindbergh had made it across the Atlantic. Well before he had left Langley for Boston, he knew this thing had ugly stamped all over it.

"Yeah, no shit. No worries on that score, buddy. We can supply one or two of our paramilitary types as backup. You remember those guys . . . and . . . those days."

I laughed out loud as I shook my head. "Forget that, Phil. Those guys are very good but I need someone I can trust with my life and who knows the area better than me."

Phil shrugged his shoulders. "You got a name?"

"Not officially, I don't."

Phil smiled. "This gonna cost us?"

"Yup."

"Just send us an invoice for the guy and Uncle Sam will cut you a check."

"Yeah, right," I answered with a bigger smile. "Like that's going to happen. This guy only takes cash."

Phil's eyes widened to the point where they were now half open instead of his usual lizard slits. "That ain't going to fly back at headquarters, Ian."

"Oh, bullshit," I said, turning serious at his response. "The Agency literally lugs around suitcases full of millions in cash all over Afghanistan to bribe warlords and they won't be able to give you a few thousand or so in cash. Give me a break."

Phil went back to smiling. "What amount is 'or so'?"

"I'll let you know."

"I bet you will."

With that necessary bit of business out of the way and with zero sincerity, I asked him back to my house for dinner. He didn't want to be around me any more than I wanted to be around him. He responded that he had a nine o'clock flight back to Washington. As we shook hands, he stared at me intently. I knew what was going through his mind. Would he ever see me alive again? Hey, I could be hit by a falling piano when I walked out of the office. But Phil and I both knew that a piano was the least of my problems.

To end our difficult and bizarre conversation, Phil launched into some predictable and always uncomfortable small talk.

"Listen, Ian. The next time you come down to Washington, I want you to promise that you'll stay with Karen and me."

I nodded. "I promise."

Phil buttoned his suit coat. As he did, I looked at the Pepsi spots that surrounded the middle button.

Phil smiled with a thought. "Come down after August, and we can check out the Redskins. I have season tickets."

I had to laugh at that one. Phil said, "I have season tickets," as if he were saying, "In my spare time I defy gravity and levitate." I was supposed to be awed by such knowledge.

"The Redskins blow, Phil. The Patriots are going to turn it around. Super Bowl here we come . . . again."

"You been sniffing that Wite-Out again, Ian? The Pats' Super Bowl years are way behind them."

The small talk was now old, and I just wanted to be left alone.

"Phil, next we'll be talking about the weather. You're going to miss your plane if you don't mush."

I opened the office door and stared blankly at the carpeted hallway. Phil cleared his throat and I looked up. He shook my hand again.

"Someone from the Agency will contact you tomorrow."

"Swell."

"Keep your head up, Ian."

"Don't worry, coach. I'll be okay, but thanks for the pep talk."

He gave me his eight-thousand-dollar smile again and walked down the hall.

I closed the door behind him, then went in and sat at my desk. What goes around, comes around, I thought. Time to go home.

7

Still stretching pennies into copper wire, I took the Orange Line to the Forest Hills T station. From there I grabbed the East Walpole local bus to Dedham center.

Dedham is a nice little suburb that borders Boston to the south. I had a small three-bedroom shanty that seemed to have the mortgage of Donald Trump's country home. I was living the American dream. I had to remind myself of that sometimes as I wrote out the check.

I lived on Endicott Street, which is just across from the Endicott estate. It's a big old yellow board and brick mansion that looks as if it belongs in a Civil War movie. Rhett Butler would look right at home standing on its front porch.

For a bachelor, I did myself pretty good in the house department. I had a one-level, redbrick "ranch-style" home with a small finished basement. My heavy oak, black-painted front door was framed by two windows on each side. Each window in turn was framed by stylish black wooden shutters whose bottoms could just be seen above my neatly trimmed green hedges. "Metrosexual" with pride, I thought, as I slid my key into the lock.

I expected my Chocolate Point Siamese cat Gizmo to come

running as I opened the front door, but then I remembered that I'd been gone for two months and if Gizmo was inside now, he would have vultures flying over his furry little body.

My sister, Janice, who still lived in the Dorchester section of Boston where we were born, was nice enough to take him while I was out of town. Her son, Patrick—my best buddy in "the whole wide universe," as we always said to each other—and Gizmo had bonded months ago, so I knew he was in the hands of an animal-loving nine-year-old.

I'd have to call and tell her to bring him back home. But not tonight. I didn't want to talk to anyone just now. I only wanted to do a short workout and sleep. It had been a long and incredibly strange day, and I only wished for the safety of sleep to end it for me.

Inside my eighteen-hundred-square-foot home, things stayed simple and neat. My living room/dining room combination was on the left side of the house, with the master bedroom with bath, and two small bedrooms and a full bath to the right. At the back of the house, situated just behind the dining room, was a very large eat-in kitchen. Behind that was a brick wall and behind that was my fairly new eight-by-twelve-foot deck. The deck looked down upon my lush backyard, recently cut by the kid down the street.

All nice and all things I was proud of, but at this moment, they were the furthest things from my mind. Right now I just desperately needed to relieve the stress of the last couple of hours.

With that in mind, I went into my bedroom, stripped to my underwear, and put on a pair of light blue running shorts. I then proceeded to work out for the next half hour. Sit-ups, push-ups, and curls with a seventy-five-pound bar. At the end of the half hour, my body was covered with a light sheen of sweat. Sweat that was hopefully taking away some of my stress along with some of my salt content.

I took a very long hot shower, brushed my teeth, put on clean underwear and a pair of black running shorts, and went to sleep.

An hour later I was still wide awake. I was getting sick of lying there in the dark and watching the red numbers on my clock change. I blamed Phil for my newfound insomnia. If he had not come to see me today, I would now be sleeping and having some type of normal horrible nightmare.

Instead I was fully awake as my mind raced with a thousand thoughts. Most of them dealt with the CIA: how I got involved with that organization, and why they came to be interested in a young man from Boston who had no interest in them.

The more I thought about it, the more I realized how simple the answer really was. *I fit their profile.* Simple. I fit the profile.

Oh, not the profile for the vast majority of their employees, the clerks, the analysts, or the management people. Not even the profile for most of their clandestine agents. I don't think I would have ever fit the profile for them. No, I wasn't quite "sane" enough for that type of work.

I was special. Apparently very special. As a matter of fact, I was so unique and gifted, I fit the profile of the candidates the Agency wanted for their Directorate of Operations or "special ops" section. The malcontents. The crazies.

What's that, you say? Got a job that's too dirty or dangerous to be handled by any of the normal people in the Agency? No problem. We'll just give it to those psychos in special ops. Who gives a rat's ass what happens to those people? They're not all there anyway.

Yeah, I fit the profile all right. Perfect made-to-order malcontent. Let's sign this bad boy up and sic him on somebody fast, before the foam dries on his mouth.

But *why* did I fit the profile? That again is a question that is fairly easy to answer. I fit their profile because life had not been so nice to me my first eighteen years on the planet. As a matter of fact, it had been quite cruel. But lucky me. According to my recruiter at the Agency, that adversity had given me this abnormal ability to think instinctively and quickly on my feet. Swell.

I had no childhood. Oh sure, I had the usual chronological childhood. I wasn't born an adult. I just had no time for fun. No time to be a kid. Something got in the way of all that. It was called abject poverty.

The reason my family had no money was that my father was an alcoholic. However, he was not your typical dipso, the kind that would sit down at the table and get drunk every night.

No. He was much worse. He would never drink when things were going bad for him. When out of money or down on his luck, he would buckle down and make a few dollars on any number of real estate scams he had going at the time. Then, once he had some money, it would come time for us to pour him home through the keyhole.

He would drink for a month at a time, run out of money, and go through the whole process all over again. That would not have been so bad except for one minor problem: Dad just hated to pay the mortgage or the rent. He considered it a monumental waste of good drinking and whoring money.

Consequently, we moved an average of twice a year for the first seventeen years of my life. Many of those moves were to different neighborhoods in our tough but beloved Dorchester.

Not exactly conducive to making lasting friendships. It was during that time that I learned there is only one thing you can count on in life. Just one thing. And that is yourself. Nobody else would ever be there for you. Nobody. At least not for me.

I had many brushes with the law during my formative years. Nothing that bad, really. I was just obsessed with beating the system, with seeing how much I could get away with. How much harder I could push. How much more clever I could be.

Things at home were not getting better. My mother, who had worked very hard to make my brother, sister, and me happy, was slowly caving in to the pressure. She in turn was, ironically and cruelly, starting to develop a severe drinking problem.

Life was not the bowl of cherries I had thought it would be when I watched *The Partridge Family* or *The Brady Bunch*. No, not at all. More like *Angela's Ashes*. Only with much less literary flair.

When I was just beginning my junior year at the fourth high school I had attended to that point, my father fell into one of his lucid periods, made some money off some various crooked deals, and moved us once again. This time it was to a very affluent town called Westwood, about forty minutes southwest of Boston and bordering Dedham.

I honestly believe that if we had not moved to Westwood, I would have ended up in prison or dead. While Dorchester was, overall, mostly filled with good, hardworking people, I was hanging around some very dangerous individuals. Most of them are now dead, or what passes for dead.

At Westwood High School I discovered something that changed my life forever. Sports. I found that all of that running I had been doing from the cops in Dorchester could be put to better use around a quarter-mile track in Westwood.

Not only that, but I quickly found out that I was bigger, stronger, and faster than most of my classmates. Presto! That in turn entices another change in people. They tend to treat you differently. Much better. You're a successful jock, so the teachers let you slide. And your classmates start treating you like you're the crown prince of the school. If high school is the breeding ground for superficiality, then high school sports is the incubator.

The more I thought about that, the more I realized that my athletic ability could be turned to a plus in the insecure "real" world.

Could I really keep it going after I got out of school? That was the question. As a very small child, I had witnessed the end of the Bobby Orr era in Boston. Only the best hockey player ever to lace up a pair of skates. The people of Beantown would have elected him Emperor of the Universe if he had run for it. Because of him, I developed an interest in hockey. After a while I grew to love the game. The competition.

I always loved to compete with anyone for anything. Friend or foe, I didn't care. Just give me the chance to win, and I would leap at it. I was then, and continue to be now, the worst loser I have ever known. It's not my most attractive trait. Regardless of what low-class behavior it brought out in me, I thought about hockey—a lot. And the more I thought about it, the more I was convinced I could make a living at it.

Every spare minute I had was spent in a hockey rink. They'd call people like me "rink rats." I would take the ice time whenever and wherever I could get it. During the summer, my friends would be going off to the beach and I would be in a hockey rink with other idiots doing wind sprints and playing pickup games.

Ultimately, the pain and sacrifice paid off. I was asked to play defense for a team in the New England Junior Hockey League. There I was noticed by a scout for the Boston Bruins. He invited me to training camp with the Bruins as a free agent. Of course, I later learned that the invite had very little to do with my marginal talent and everything to do with my large size for a hockey player and my street-honed ability to land a punch. The Bruins were in the market for a lowbrow goon, and I fit the bill.

Once at camp, I was assigned to the Bruins' American Hockey League affiliate. I was twenty years old and got my brains beat in. For three days the game was tag, and I was it.

After those three days, I was cut in a very impersonal way. The assistant coach posted the names of the players going on a road trip to play in Halifax, Nova Scotia. If your name was not on the list, "kindly and quickly leave training camp." Not finding my name on the list, I started packing to go home. As I did, the scout who had given me my chance, and really believed in me, pulled me aside and said: "Ian, no matter what else you do in life, finish college. It will always give you something to fall back on."

I knew all too well how right he was. I was not counting on being the next Bobby Orr. I was going to cover my ass, and that meant getting the sheepskin. My major in college was political science. Soviet studies. It was during that time that I first heard from the Agency. They somehow managed to send a letter to my home before the next eviction. It read:

Dear Mr. Wallace:

It has come to my attention that your background may be of employment interest to the Central Intelligence Agency.

Before an appointment to this Agency is made, it is usually necessary to complete: a local interview, completion of formal applications, testing, background investigations, and headquarters interviews. In all, it generally requires 80–120 days after our local interview before we can make a formal employment commitment.

Please call this office to establish an interview date in Boston. Should any of these procedures preclude your interest or availability, please let me know. I hope this letter may be an initial step in exploring a rewarding and challenging career.

Sincerely yours,
Charles Prosky

At first I thought the letter was a practical joke perpetrated by my cousin Steve. He was always punking me one way or the other, and a letter from the CIA would more than fit the pattern. Once I figured out it was genuine, I stuck it in the mirror above my dresser (which was missing two drawers) and just stared at it from time to time.

I never thought much about working for the government, or anyone for that matter. Hey, what did I care. Even though I had just been cut by the Bruins, I was still going to try to play hockey for a living. Who needed a real job?

The really bad thing about saying "who needs a real job" is that the rest of the world demands you do real work, inherit money, resort to crime, or starve. Just when you think you have it made, reality has a way of knocking on your front door and saying "One order of severe pain. Hold the dream."

One year after being cut by the Bruins' farm team, I was lucky enough to be invited to training camp by the New York Rangers. I was twenty-one years old, had my college degree, and was ready to prove myself. It was there that "reality" re-introduced itself by tapping me rather rudely on the shoulder, or right knee to be precise, and decided to destroy my marginal shot at playing a kids' game for a living.

As camp started, all I could think was, Let me at 'em, coach. I'll make them wish they took up chess instead of hockey. Well, they did let me at 'em. We were playing the New York Islanders in an exhibition game at Madison Square Garden in New York. I was playing right defense at the time. I was just starting to carry the puck out of our zone when reality hit me with a check on my right leg. Not too bad, I thought. I've been hit harder.

Yes, that is exactly what reality wanted me to think. Because what I didn't know was that reality was far from finished with the check. As it hit me, my right leg went backward and up in the air. While it was up there, my right skate got caught in the top of the boards and stayed there. Reality saw this and decided that then was a good time to fall, full force, in the guise of a 220-pound player, on my right knee. I'm told they could hear the pop my knee made up in the twentieth row of the Garden.

It was six months before I could put on skates again. And it was a total waste of time. I tried to play in the lowest minor league in professional hockey and could not even keep up there. My knee was gone. Blown out at the ripe old age of twenty-one. Good-bye, dream; hello, cruel world.

For a while there, I was really starting to feel sorry for myself. Whatever was I going to do with myself? It was during that time that I once again heard from the Agency. They were nothing if not persistent and patient. They said they could still offer me a career, travel, excitement, and the chance to serve my country, so why not sign up?

What the hell, I thought, a job is a job. Wrong again. I was starting to become an expert at being wrong, an expertise that did not seem to be a marketable skill unless you were a weatherman, an economist, or a political pundit.

The following week, I took a city bus to the local T station and then took the T to the State Street train station in downtown Boston. No surprise, I was going to the John F. Kennedy Federal Building, located next to City Hall.

I was half hoping that, like Maxwell Smart from the old *Get Smart* television series, I would walk through a series of doors that slammed closed behind me until I got to the phone booth at the end, where I would dial a special number and drop through the floor, down a tube, and be on my way to my secret appointment.

No such luck. I walked into the building and took the elevator to the twelfth floor, then walked into a nondescript office suite and saw a nondescript receptionist. I gave my name and was told to take a seat.

No sooner had I started to flip through the latest *Sports Illustrated* than Mr. P poked his head out of his office and called for me.

I walked into his office and closed the door behind me. Again I was greeted with disappointment. No "cone of silence," no secret gadgets, and no Bat Phone. I was starting to have serious doubts regarding my years of research.

Mr. P. was fairly tall, thin, well dressed, had thick salt-and-pepper hair, and looked like a Hollywood version of an Ivy League professor. At least I still had *that* part right. He directed me to one of the two chairs in front of his desk.

To the best of my recollection, the conversation went something like this:

"Thank you for coming in," he said.

"You're welcome. I guess I only have one question before we start. And that is—"

Mr. P. cut me off. "Why you?"

I nodded and said nothing.

"Mr. Wallace. Ian. Do you mind if I'm totally frank with you?"

Nothing good ever comes behind a question like that, but I again nodded my head.

He clapped his hands together and began. "Good. Let me give you a thumbnail sketch of things and then answer why we reached out to you."

I actually found myself inching forward in my seat. Both out of curiosity and in case I had to bolt out the door should the situation become more surreal than it already was.

"My job," he began, "is to find two types of employee for the Central Intelligence Agency. The first is the analyst type. You know, the ones who work at headquarters and analyze the millions of bits of information that come pouring in every day. By far, the analyst positions represent the largest percentage of our employees."

The more I inched forward in my chair, the more he leaned back in his very comfortable-looking black leather chair. Maybe I should have had a mint before coming into the office.

"The second position, the one that is always inaccurately

portrayed in movies and books, is that of a field agent. Meaning, of course, someone who works in our clandestine service overseas, generally under cover, and gathers information that is critical to the defense of the United States. It is that position, and our need to fill some openings, that brings you here today."

I decided on the spot that I really didn't want to know *why* they suddenly had openings to fill. My imagination was in fine working order. Sitting before Mr. P. in the Boston field office of the Central Intelligence Agency had automatically shifted my imagination into fifth gear. Details I could do without.

"So, why me for *that* position?" I managed to croak out.

He folded his hands before him on his desk and smiled at me. "Again, Ian. Is it all right if I'm perfectly honest with you?"

"Yes, sir," I answered.

He nodded his head and continued. "Because, to put it as bluntly as possible, you're a complete head-case, your family life is screwed up, and near as I can tell, your future is preordained to fail."

Wow, I thought. Had I known *that* was a qualification for government work, I would have started screwing things up years earlier. Maybe I could have been in Congress by now.

He continued. "Without naming names, a former professor of yours brought your situation to our attention. Since then we've kept an eye on you. And what we've seen indicates to us that you would operate well in the field."

What's that? I thought. That I look like Pig-Pen from *Peanuts* on most days and could therefore be invisible to the enemy? That's what I *thought*. What I said was "Why?"

"Why? Because you've dealt with just about every bit of misfortune life can throw at you at a young age, and you keep surviving. No matter what the situation, or how quickly it changes, you adapt. You adapt, you learn, and you grow stronger. There are few people we've seen who think faster on their feet than you. All qualifications that would make for an excellent field agent."

Perfect. So all this time I thought Mom and Dad were destroying my life with neglect and poverty, when in reality they were establishing my qualifications for dangerous government work in faraway lands. I made a mental note to thank them when they sobered up.

After a few more minutes of dazed conversation, I left the office and made my way back home with the promise that I would call him in a few days.

Weeks passed as I considered my options. On a blank piece of paper I listed said options. On the right side I listed the CIA. On the left side I listed all my other options. Zero. The big goose egg.

Okay. Decision made. I wanted out of my horrible existence in the worst way possible, and the CIA was throwing me a lifeline. I decided to grab on with both hands and let it drag me away from my pathetic life.

Once I informed them of my decision, the Agency put me through a very intense and lengthy background check. One of the things that most amused me about the background check was that even though they were bringing me in to work in the "covert" side of the Agency, the investigators who interviewed my family, friends, and former coworkers were only too happy to announce that they were with the CIA. So much for keeping my future occupation a secret.

8

_____

Once they were satisfied that I was a good, if twisted American, they had me report to an office building in downtown Rosslyn, Virginia, for my physical. After two days of being turned into a human pin cushion, and having Doctors put their fingers in places I'd rather not think about, it was off to headquarters.

I have to admit, as blasé as I wanted to pretend I was about the whole thing, I was fairly excited about the prospect of actually going to the super-secret headquarters of the Central Intelligence Agency. Like the vast majority of Americans, I had only seen it on television programs, the movies, or in the news. Not only was I about to drive through the front gates, but inexplicably, they wanted me to work for them.

Seeing the main building for the first time did not disappoint. It was both impressive and intimidating. As we walked into the front entrance, our "keeper" took great pains to point out the seal of the Central Intelligence Agency ingrained in granite beneath our feet. After allowing us to look at the seal for a few seconds, so our minds could fully realize that we were truly at the American James Bond factory, it was off to visit the lie detector machines.

Together with about fifteen other candidates, including a former air force fighter pilot, a former Green Beret, and a Secret Service agent, the lowlife from Dorchester walked away from the seal and down the hallway for a two-hour polygraph.

As it turned out, the examiner I got was not an altogether normal guy. He felt it necessary to do a card trick for me. He put a blood pressure cuff on my arm, hooked up my fingertips, and put that cord around my chest.

"Now, Mr. Wallace," the rodent-looking man said in a mind-numbing monotone, "I'm going to show you why it is a total waste of time trying to lie to us."

He then gave me a deck of cards and asked me to pick one out, look at it, and put it back in the deck.

Once done, he then named off every card in the deck and asked if it was my card. I was instructed to say no every time, thereby exposing my lie. Well, sure enough, he got me. He looked at his little graph paper and said: "Your card is the two of spades."

I just smiled up at him. "Hey, no shit? Listen, let me ask you a question. Does David Copperfield know you're doing his act?"

This guy may have had great confidence in his machine and his ability to interpret the squiggles it produced, but soon after the exam, I found out that it was subjectively accurate. It depended in large measure upon the person taking the test, and his or her ability to tell the truth, lie, or be influenced by nerves.

After taking the test, I was left alone in the room for about a half hour to contemplate life. As I continued my rather pedestrian thought process, the supervisor of the lie detector technician walked in to announce in a very loud voice that I had failed the test. As my career of last resort burst into flames before my eyes, I managed to squeak out, "How? Why? I didn't lie about jack shit."

He smiled back at me with the look of someone who had just stopped a crime in progress.

"Drugs," he said as he energetically nodded his thin head up and down. "You lied to us about your past drug use."

"What?" I screamed. "Look, dickhead, you're the one on drugs if you think I ever used drugs."

I was more than ready to go down for something I had done wrong, but I had never done drugs in my life. Not once. Not ever.

After continued earnest protesting on my part, they re-tested me and determined that because, as a teen, I had hung around hard-core drug users—and even held the spoon for them as they melted their heroin over an open flame—these background activities had caused me to fail the "drug use" part of the exam.

Maybe my subconscious was just trying to get me out of a job that was about to infuse me with a lifetime of pain. I later wished that it had tried harder.

9

Weeks later, after they had made sure we all passed muster and washed behind our ears, we were packed onto a little blue bus. Next destination: "the Farm." Its real name is Camp Peary. Well, actually, that's not quite right, either. Camp Peary is just the fake name for the fake military base we trained at, located near the real Williamsburg, Virginia.

Toward the end of my training at the Farm, I heard that Delta Force—the elite United States commando team inspired by the Israeli and West German commando units that staged very successful hostage rescues at Entebbe and Mogadishu airports, respectively—was looking to the agency for some paramilitary "volunteers." I was instantly intrigued and wanted in for a number of reasons. I expected to encounter nothing but hostility from the Agency when I expressed my desire to join this team.

Much to my surprise, delight, and suspicion, however, they agreed completely. They felt the extra training would be a great benefit to me and them in the long run. Even better, it would save them a great deal of money should they want me for their own paramilitary unit later in my career. So, with their self-interested blessing, I packed my bags and headed farther south to Fort Bragg, North Carolina. Home of all things "Special Forces," "Special Ops," and "Special Scary."

This incredibly elite and patriotic collection of operatives had come to the attention of the American people about a decade earlier because of the "failed" Iran hostage rescue mission.

During conversations I had at the Agency about this team, I located an instructor who had been involved in that heroic and valiant effort. He in turn had often wondered out loud if the mission had in fact "failed" because the White House had rushed the operation so the president could disgustingly attach himself to a successful rescue and thereby bask in the positive press coverage needed to help defeat his well-known and momentum-building opponent in the Democratic primaries.

No matter the actual motivations, the indisputable truth was that eight selfless and courageous Americans lost their lives on a remote makeshift landing strip in the Iranian desert. A tragic lesson was forever learned by our warfighters regarding the deadly and often doomed mixing of politics and combat.

How easy it was for old politicians and civilian policy makers who had never served their nation in uniform or been near a combat operation to send young men and women into battle and oftentimes certain death. If done for political or partisan reasons, then it was nothing less than a betrayal of those troops.

10

Upon arrival, I was introduced to the commander of the commando unit, a gentleman by the name of Colonel William Buckworth. The colonel stood about six feet, five inches tall, weighed about 240 pounds, and made the Marlboro Man's face look as smooth as a baby's bottom. The man was quite intimidating in his fatigues, combat boots, and green beret as he stood before me and caused a partial eclipse of the sun.

Being a Yankee and foolishly thinking I was clever, I smiled at the colonel and asked, in my best "Paaak the Caaa in Haavaad Yaaad" Boston accent, if after my training was complete, he might see fit to bring me to Mayberry, North Carolina, so I might meet Andy, Aunt Bea, Opie, Barney Fife, and Otis?

He nodded his head up and down and looked at the equally large captain from Special Forces standing to my right, and then back at me.

"Well, I'll tell you what, fuckface. I'm gonna do better than that. I'm gonna introduce you to this dirt in front of me. Get your Yankee turd ass down there and give me fifty."

Obviously, the man did not have a sense of humor.

"Hey, look, Colonel. It was only a jo—"

Before I could finish the sentence, the captain swept my feet out from under me. As I hit the ground, he planted his right boot on the back of my neck, grabbed my left hand, and pulled my arm up toward my head. It was not a fun experience.

"Listen, boy, the colonel just asked you to do something. Now are you gonna do fifty or do I pull your arm out of its socket?"

It's very hard to address a person when your face is being pushed into the North Carolina topsoil by 230 pounds of Green Beret, but I tried.

"Tell you what, pussy. Why don't you let me up from here, and I'll show you how we do fifty back in Boston."

He actually giggled as he released his grip on me. Maybe I should have taken that as an omen. As I started to get up, the captain caught me full force with his steel-toed boot in the solar plexus. The wind exploded from me like the Hindenburg going up on a grainy newsreel. Back down I went to get reacquainted with the pleasingly cool dirt.

The colonel then leaned down to talk to me as I wheezed like an octogenarian finishing the Boston Marathon.

"We all appreciate a good joke now and then, Mr. Wallace. But in this unit you have to earn the right first. To use a vernacular you might better understand, you're just a rookie in this league. Let's see if you can make it through our little training camp before you start telling your shit-ass jokes."

As he and the captain started to walk away, he turned back and said, "Oh, and by the way, turd, after you catch your breath, I still want fifty before you get back on your feet."

Several very smart answers ran through my mind. I picked the one that would instill the most fear in him. "Yes, sir," I said.

* * *

After our initial disagreement over my material, the colonel and I got along fine. He just wanted to get his message across. He was the boss, and I was a bug to be squashed for his perverse pleasure. Once I had that concept down, the rest was easy.

The colonel was a very bad dude who had run many a clandestine operation in Vietnam. It was there that he earned his reputation for arrogance and contempt for ignorant superiors. I quickly realized that I could learn a great deal from this man who hid a great intellect beneath a veneer of all too real, but exaggerated, toughness.

When they were putting the unit together, the colonel said that he wanted just three things from his people: "I want men who are highly intelligent, in great physical condition, and can keep their mouths shut." I had the great physical condition part covered, as well as keeping my trap shut. "Highly intelligent" was a requirement I was going to have to fake.

The training I and my colleagues endured went on for weeks in various elements of marksmanship, pain, lock-picking, pain, demolition training, pain, surveillance and countersurveillance, and pain until we finally achieved some degree of proficiency.

Once we felt we were ready, we put on little demonstrations for select supervisors and officials. At one of the compounds, we had interior mock-ups of airplanes and trains. And special rooms we would use for target practice.

We would ask the officials to go into these rooms and rearrange the targets, which were just a series of life-size pasteboard photographs of figures, in groups of twos and threes. They could choose those who they wanted to be "terrorists."

Once they chose their terrorists, they gave them pasteboard weapons.

We would then ask them to stand in the back of the room behind a protective shield and shut off all the lights. Total darkness. We, of course, were outside and did not know who they chose to be the bad guys or where they chose to position them.

No problem. We just broke down the door and for the next twenty seconds there would be multiple muzzle flashes and the metallic sound of silenced automatic weapons and pistol fire as the room filled with smoke and the smell of spent rounds.

Colonel Buckworth would then snap on the lights and there we were. Dressed in night fighting gear, special night-vision goggles—now resting on our foreheads—and laser pointers attached to our weapons. As we looked around the room, we smiled to ourselves because every "terrorist" had multiple rounds in the K-5 killing zone, which was basically anything from the head down to the belt buckle. Not a scratch on the good guys. The truth of the matter was that we could do that ten times out of ten. Perfect.

After training, I went back to Boston to see my family for the next two weeks. Instead of two weeks, I had to settle for two days. No sooner was I at my mother's small apartment than I got a call asking me to report back to Bragg on the double.

I explained to my mother that I had to fly back down to Washington, D.C., to do some more work. She never pressed me about my job, but I could see the fear in her eyes as I kissed her good-bye. I honestly felt guilty for causing such pain in a woman who had been running scared all of her adult life. But nothing I now said would relieve her tension. She wanted me to stay, but that was the one thing I could not do. I had finally found a purpose in life and a like-minded group of individuals and friends who needed, earned, and deserved my commitment to our common cause of protecting our nation and her citizens from the growing list of enemies outside our borders.

On the commercial flight back to North Carolina, a million thoughts ran through my mind. A million scenarios. What could be wrong? Once at the meeting, Colonel Buckworth ended all the speculation.

The shit was hitting the fan with extreme prejudice down in Panama, to the point where the thug and dictator Manuel Noriega, in the guise of the killers, drug dealers, and mercenaries he employed in his personal army of "Dignity Battalions," had actually started to take hostages and kill United States military personnel.

Not on our watch, *Señor Dickhead.*

Almost all of the operations being directed against our people were being planned and executed out of a Panama Defense Forces garrison in Rio Hato and the *La Comandancia* central headquarters of the PDF in downtown Panama. As Operation Just Cause was swinging into action, our team was asked to assist in the targeting of these installations.

Simply put, our orders were to find the snakes ordering the kidnapping, torture, and killing of our people and deal with them in one of two ways: take them into custody upon surrender or exterminate them like vermin should they so much as look at us in a menacing way.

Our team took no one into custody.

II

After the mission, the Agency changed course in midstream and felt its plans would be better suited if I were once again among their ranks in an official way. The world was changing fast. Almost too fast. The Berlin Wall had just fallen. Panama had just flared up and had to be tamped down in our own hemisphere. What was next?

So, after a couple of weeks of downtime at home in Boston, it was back down to the puzzle palace in Langley for reassignment.

The assignment I received was the American embassy in Moscow. I could not have been happier with their choice.

With my background in Soviet studies, you would think that it would only make sense for the Agency to send me there. You would think that, and you would be wrong. But you would be wrong for the right reason. And that is, you would be making sense. Making sense and the Agency do not always go hand in hand. I could just as easily have ended up in Venezuela.

At that time, the Soviet Union—at the very end of its Cold War existence—and the United States played a perpetual game of cat and mouse. When one of our agents went into Moscow, the Soviets pretty much knew he or she was employed by the CIA, and not by the State Department or another government agency as claimed.

At the same time, we always knew who was KGB and who was not when they entered the United States. The game began when one side tried to keep tabs on the other. And in that respect, the Soviet Union had a clear advantage.

In a closed society such as the former Soviet Union, it was a fairly simple procedure to follow those you believed to be CIA operatives, since the vast majority of the country was off-limits to American nationals. In the United States, however, it was unbelievably easy for the Soviets to get around undetected. It is said that freedom has many prices, as we have since learned the hard way. Knowing that still didn't make the FBI counterintelligence unit's life any easier. But I did and do sympathize.

My job was to try to get Soviet citizens to supply us with whatever information they could gather that was counterproductive to the Soviet Union. When I sat alone at night and gave it any real thought, the idea sickened me a little. What I was asking these people to do, in reality, was to sell out their nation. Whether it was for money, sex, drugs, or political reasons, it was still selling out. And it felt wrong. Dirty. And no matter how many showers I took, it was a filth that was always going to be with me for as long as I had a memory.

We were creating "traitors," and when doing so, sometimes things go wrong. Incredibly wrong. In most professions, when something goes wrong, you get lectured, or worst case, fired. In my world, when something you were working on went south, usually one of two things happened: either you got killed, or the person you were turning against their country got tortured and killed. More often than not it was the latter. But no matter which one, it made for a very bad day.

We were constantly aware that one slip-up on our part could and would have the most dire consequences. The only question was how much pain would be inflicted.

In my first month in Moscow I had been greeted by just such a grim example. Alan Marshall, a covert agent who had been in Moscow for two years and was rotating back to Langley, had been in an especially good mood since my arrival.

First, because my presence meant he could go home, and second, because he was on the verge of one of the biggest "turns" in Agency history. For almost eighteen months, Alan had been working a KGB major who not only wanted to defect to the United States with his wife and three-year-old daughter, but also was privy to the list of every KGB undercover agent working in America.

If Alan and the Agency could get their hands on that list, it would set the KGB back decades. They would need a telescope just to see forward to the Stone Age.

Everything was going incredibly well until Alan got a call at 4 a.m. asking him to be in front of the U.S. embassy in thirty minutes.

As soon as he hung up, Alan called me. As I lived closer, I got to the embassy before him. Five minutes later, he ran up to me out of breath and sweating despite the five-below Moscow temperature.

"What's up?" I asked.

He pulled the black wool skullcap tighter down over his ears and then jammed his hands back into the pockets of his navy peacoat.

"Beats the fuck out of me," he hissed as a white frost cloud escaped his mouth. "All I know is that it was an Ivan, and that the guy's voice made the hair on the back of my neck stand on end."

"Ivan" was our nickname for KGB agents. Just as I was about to say something, a black Russian ZIL pulled up directly in front of us.

I looked over at Alan and smiled. "Did you order Domino's?"

He did not even bother to acknowledge me. His entire being was riveted on the black curtains that covered the inside of the back windows of the ZIL.

After what seemed like hours, but was only two minutes, the rear driver's-side curtain was pulled aside and the window was rolled down, and both Alan and I caught a glimpse of a broad white smile with a glint of chrome in the middle of a face that looked to be chiseled out of marble.

No sooner did we see the smile and face than the window was rolled back up and the ZIL took off at a high rate of speed. It was seconds before it dawned on us that the passenger had dropped something out of the window onto the snow-packed street. The something was a black duffel bag.

As Alan and I walked up to it, we noticed the snow around the bottom of the bag turning red.

Alan stopped in his tracks and cried out, "It's Dmitri!"

"Who?" I asked, feeling more and more apprehensive.

Alan leaned down, grabbed the top of the duffel bag, opened it, and looked down toward the bottom. A few seconds later, a lone tear followed his gaze to the bottom of the black bag.

I leaned over and looked for myself. Just as quickly, I jumped back in panic and disgust. I could feel my gag reflex trigger as I fought not to throw up on the street. Staring up from the bottom of the bag was the head of a thirty-something man with bright blue eyes open wide in a terror that I could only imagine.

Alan started hyperventilating and collapsed next to the bag. "It's the KGB major. My 'turn.' The bastards cut off his fuckin' head."

Alan then started to rock back and forth screaming, "I'm so sorry!" over and over again. He was still screaming it as two United States Marines helped me carry him into the grounds of the embassy.

As we half carried, half dragged him inside, the black bag he held in a death grip in his right hand left an evenly spaced series of red dots on the snow.

My initiation into the horrors of Moscow began at that moment, but the worst was yet to come.

12

---

everal months later, while working night and day to get Soviets of
stature to rat out everything they believed in, I violated
one of the oldest rules in the business: Do not get emo-
tionally involved with your operatives. I violated this rule in a
big way. I fell in love.

I will always have a passion for hockey, for the ice. It was
this fascination for the sport that started to complicate my
somewhat simple life. During what little free time I had, I used
to enjoy going over to the sports center and watching the Red
Army and Dynamo national hockey teams practice and play.
During one of my trips there, I arrived earlier than usual and
was greeted with the sight of twenty or thirty female figure
skaters going through their practice routines.

Since reaching puberty, I have always been a sucker for
dancers and figure skaters. They have, by far, as a collective
group, the most beautiful bodies on the planet. Their most
eye-catching features are their legs and backsides. This particular group was no exception.

As I sat and tried not to look like a pervert on parole, I noticed one above all others. She was gorgeous. Breathtakingly
beautiful, with an incredibly strong body. If she had even one

ounce of fat on her body, she did a truly remarkable job of hiding it.

She had light blond hair piled high on top of her head and tied with a blue ribbon. She wore a royal blue skating outfit with flesh-colored nylons. Over the nylons she had on bright yellow leg warmers pulled up just above her knees. Being a skater, I was amazed at how effortlessly she moved across the ice. An artist in every sense of the word.

From that moment on, I made a point of always going to the sports center early to catch her skating. As the weeks progressed, we began to talk. She spoke English very well, which more than made up for my halting Russian. She told me that her name was Irena, and that she had noticed me many times sitting up there in the stands. I explained to her that I worked at the American embassy for the United States Department of State.

She confessed to me one night, over hot chocolate at a small café down the street from the sports center, that she had always had a very strong desire to go to the United States. To stay there forever. Her next words put me in a very awkward position. She said she would be willing to trade information for her freedom.

She was an analyst working at Moscow University. And the project she was currently working on was analyzing test data from the Sary Shagan proving ground in the central part of the USSR. I nearly fell off my chair with that bit of information. Sary Shagan was where the Soviet Union tested their "directed energy weapons," meaning laser and particle beams, as well as X-ray beam technology. They were also testing kinetic energy devices such as railguns at Sary Shagan.

All of these things would be employed in their own "Star

Wars" space-based defense systems. To further exacerbate my dilemma was the fact that the Soviet Union was said to be about five years ahead of us in that field.

My problem was basic. I was starting to feel strongly about this woman and did not want to expose her to the many dangers involved with collecting information for the United States.

On the other hand, it was information the Agency was desperate to obtain. And there I was, having it handed to me on a silver platter. I told her it was something I would have to think about, and would give her an answer in a day or two.

That night, in her Spartan two-room apartment, we made passionate love for the first time. As a very spiritual man, I did not believe in indiscriminate sex. I felt it only served to cheapen both parties. That said, my job and our current circumstances did not afford us the luxury of making our love "legal." My opinion then and now is that the Lord puts true love before a paper signed by the state.

When we were spent, I turned to look at her and noticed that her cheeks were wet with tears that reflected the pale white light, which streamed in through her bedroom window from the streetlight outside. Irena put her head on my chest and wept. I wasn't quite sure why she was crying, and I was too afraid to ask. I had never made love to her before, so these were uncharted waters for me. I hoped it was because she was happy, but I knew better.

She was seeing a light at the end of the tunnel. And that light was me. As I lay there and stroked her soft blond hair, I made up my mind. The information was just too important to do without. I would have my cake and eat it, too. In the morning, I told her of my decision.

As I spoke, her deep brown eyes radiated a light of their very own. She smiled so hard I thought her face was going to break. As she ran to jump on me, I braced myself, but to no avail. We both went crashing to the floor.

We made love again that morning, right there on the rug. Only this time there were no tears. Just laughs and smiles. I was truly in love with this woman.

Over the course of the next three months, I had pretty much moved into Irena's apartment full-time as we planned our marriage and our future together.

The information she was supplying to us was incredible. It was a major coup for the Agency and for me. During this time, Irena took it upon herself to share some rather personal information with just me. She was going to have a baby.

From the way she braced herself when she told me, I think she figured I was going to get angry. When that didn't happen, she smiled. I found myself not only smiling right back, but crying. I was ecstatic. I felt truly blessed with the news.

13

The next morning, while feeling even more blessed, I was also starting to get more nervous by the minute. My trepidation had nothing to do with the miracle from God that was now establishing residence in Irena's womb, but rather with the fact that I had let her talk me into meeting her parents later that morning. How and why did I let *that* happen?

Boston, Moscow, or the North Pole, it did not matter. If you were a guy, meeting the parents of your girlfriend or fiancée was never near the top of your list of things to do. Ever.

Almost every guy I had known facing that situation had dreaded the moment. Not so much because they wouldn't like the parents, as they almost always did, but because every guy knows that the minute Mom and Dad catch sight of them, they are being put under the "Is he a dirtbag" microscope.

While the man might, if he was really, really good, be able to snow the mom into believing he mostly kept his elbows off the table, made a minimal amount of bodily noises, and chewed with his mouth closed, there was still nothing he could do or say to win over the dad. Nothing.

The dad's a guy. He knows your ultimate intentions and if he had his way, he'd be cutting things off your body and then locking the eunuch rest of you in a dungeon for the next five or six decades. Nothing personal, of course, but he's a guy. Worse, he's the *dad* and sooner or later, you are going to deflower his precious daughter. "Daddy's little girl."

Or in my case, *had* deflowered. And even though my intentions, my faith, and my love were pure, this was still the Soviet Union and different rules applied.

Irena's parents lived in a very rural area forty miles to the north of Moscow. I've seen Frankenstein movies. I know all about pitchforks, torches, and angry town folk demanding to see the monster. If, as I strongly suspected, Irena had at least already told her mom about our news, then there was no way I was not getting a pitchfork in my ass or my back peppered with rock salt as daddy let loose with both barrels of his shotgun.

Of course, as that probable scenario bounced around inside my head on the drive to her parents' home, I couldn't betray one ounce of nervousness or worry to Irena. Taking *that* fork in the road usually only produced the silent treatment, tears, or both.

Surprisingly—at least to me—I had a great time. Wonderful.

While her parents still most likely came to the conclusion that there was no way I was good enough for their daughter, I did garner some initial brownie points. The first was that I could speak passable Russian. Second, it was clear to anyone paying attention that I was head over heels in love with Irena. Apparently her mom was paying attention, since she almost instantly pulled her daughter aside to whisper into her ear while smiling and pointing at me.

While her dad may have been deliberately oblivious to my incurable infatuation with Irena, he was impressed with one thing about me: the fact that I used to play professional hockey back in the United States. After fifteen minutes of discussion, we both quickly agreed that the two best hockey players in the history of the sport were Bobby Orr of the Boston Bruins and Valeri Kharlamov of CSKA Moscow.

Not by coincidence, Irena had told me to bring my skates for the trip and I was glad she did. Two hundred feet or so behind her parents' house was a small, extremely frozen pond almost exactly the size of a hockey rink. It was there that Irena, her dad, her twelve-year-old brother, Dmitri, and I played an informal game of pickup hockey. It was me and Dmitri against Irena and her dad.

I don't think I had ever laughed so hard in my life as Irena tried every dirty trick she could think of to take the puck away from me. Slashing, holding, hooking, and even a not so gentle bite on my nose were all part of her repertoire. She made the Hanson brothers from the movie *Slap Shot* look like Gandhi wannabes by comparison.

As stunning and intelligent as she was, she was still a top-flight athlete and like most, hated to lose much more than she liked to win. Exceptional athletes expected to win and were usually shocked—or angry with less talented teammates—when they lost. Informal and fun or not, Irena was looking for an edge.

Mama didn't raise no fool and I was not about to let me and Dmitri beat her and her dad. That said, I still wanted to prove I was not a totally whipped and spineless male, so I did hip-check Irena into a fairly fluffy snowbank when the opportunity presented itself.

As her upper body disappeared into the four-foot-high pile of snow, Dmitri and her dad could barely stand on their skates as they howled with laughter and pointed at her legs scissoring wildly in the air. By the time I got to Irena and pulled her out of the snow, their loud and infectious laughter had me going as well.

Once out of the snowbank, Irena looked at the tears of laughter instantly freezing on my face and her nostrils flared with the sight. As she continued to brush the snow from her hair and upper body, she suddenly stopped, pointed to the woods behind the house, and yelled in English, "Look!"

As I turned to look, she shoved me from behind and I tumbled into the snowbank she had just vacated. The next thing I heard was her rich laugh as she giggled out "Rookie" while skating away.

14

My world fell apart exactly one week later.

I was walking by myself across Red Square at midnight when it happened. Late at night is when it is best to see Red Square. No tourists. No hassles. Just tranquility. I very much enjoyed going there at night to walk and collect my thoughts. The history of the square is awe-inspiring. The architecture is breathtaking.

Just as I stopped to take it all in, two very large men fell in step beside me. It took no stroke of genius on my part to realize that they were KGB.

The taller of the two stopped and took my left arm. "If you please, Mr. Wallace. We wish you to get into car. We want no trouble from you, please."

He pointed to a generic black ZIL sedan that had magically pulled up in front of us, its rear door wide open.

I already knew the answer to the question, but I gave it a shot anyway. "What if I don't want to go?"

The shorter one shoved me toward the car with a look of pure hatred on his face. "We kill you here."

I got into the car and smiled at the taller of the two agents as he climbed in beside me.

"I think I like you better."

That didn't seem to impress him, because he pulled a black hood out from under his gray top coat and yanked it down over my head.

"That's it," I said. "I just changed my mind. I don't like you, either." That comment got me a quick punch in the head from one of them. I couldn't see which, but I would have bet it was the short one.

"You know," I told him, "I think you exhibit such violent tendencies because you resent being a short little bastard with a tiny penis. Don't worry about it, though; it's nothing that three months with a psychiatrist and five thousand dollars can't cure."

The taller one grabbed my hood and spoke.

"You may have your laugh now, Mr. Wallace. But I think it is we who will be laughing soon."

The drive did not take long, and I knew exactly where we were going. KGB headquarters in Moscow. Please don't let this have anything to do with Irena, I prayed. The car came to a stop, and I could hear the metallic sound of a garage door going up. Once the noise stopped, the car continued forward. It now made the sounds one usually associates with the inside of a parking garage. Of course, I have never driven around a parking garage with a hood pulled down over my head, but I was still pretty sure.

The car stopped, the doors opened, and I was dragged out. I was ushered down a very long corridor. We made a right turn and then a sharp left. I was pushed through a door into what I sensed was a room. I was then brought over and forced to sit in a metal chair.

After I was slammed down into the chair, my arms and legs

were fastened to it. I was going nowhere. And neither was the chair. It was bolted to the floor.

Once I was strapped in, they removed my hood. I've seen worse. I've lived in worse. I was seated in the back of a very dark room that seemed to measure about fifteen feet by thirty. There was one light in the room. It was suspended from the ceiling by a black cord about three feet in length, and had a metallic green lampshade around it. It looked like it should have been hanging over a poker table during the Roaring Twenties. Al Capone would have loved it. Give him another place to hang one of his pals.

At the opposite end of the room from me was a single black door. And through this door walked one of the biggest men I had ever seen in my life.

The others in the room, the two KGB agents and the two GRU uniformed guards, seemed to shrink back into the wood-work as he entered. I had always considered myself to be a fairly large person, at six feet, three inches and 196 pounds, but this guy was causing me to rethink that opinion.

He was at least six feet, six inches tall and must have weighed in at a rock-hard 275 pounds at a minimum. All of this seemed magnified by the black greatcoat he wore, which came all the way down to the top of his shiny black boots. I was amazed that he had made it through the door at all. He had short brown hair and deep black eyes. His nose was flat against his face and looked as if it had been broken on more than one occasion. The most striking feature about his face was a white scar that ran from just under his right eye to the bottom of his chin. I had seen those types of scars before. It had been made by a knife.

He walked ever so slowly toward me. Each step was

deliberate. Each footstep seemed to accelerate the rate of my heartbeat. There was an evil about this man. An evil that was exuded by his mere presence in the room.

He stopped in front of my chair and looked down at me.

"Don't tell me," I said. "Let me guess. You're from the Moscow welcome wagon."

I did not see his arm move as the back of his hand caught me across the face. If I had not been strapped in, and if the chair were not bolted to the floor, then I'm sure I would have crashed against the far wall from the force of the blow. The power of the man was immense. The familiar taste of copper was in my mouth as the blood flowed from where my lips and the inside of my cheek had torn on my teeth. I tried to spit the blood on his nice shiny boots, but it ran down the outside of my chin. Just like old times in the dentist's office.

He laughed and said, "That was a very good try, Ian."

His calling me by my first name was supposed to establish who was in charge. It was one of the first things they taught us at the Farm. During an interrogation, always call your prisoner by his or her first name. It will demoralize them. I wonder if Ivan had the same instructors I did? In this business, you never knew.

He grabbed me by my hair and jerked my head up. "My name is Colonel Vladimir Ivanchenko. I am a Soviet policeman. And you, Ian, are an American spy."

There was something very different about this guy. Something not quite right. Not in synch with the rest of humanity. Then I had it: It was his eyes. They seemed not to reflect the light. As if they were flat. They seemed psychotic. They were eyes that scared me. Eyes that held my attention.

"Now tell us, Ian, what are you doing in Moscow?"

I tried to look nonchalant. It was not working.

"I'm in Moscow with the State Department. I'm just here to deal with tourists and their travel problems and help out with the paperwork back at the embassy. You know, low-level clerk stuff."

He smiled down at me. His left eyetooth was chrome. My mind immediately flashed back to that night in front of the U.S. embassy. Same person. It was a smile of evil then, but it was something much worse now. Maybe my head was about to end up at the bottom of a bag.

He took my left arm and turned it up so that my wrist was facing the ceiling. He then pulled his hand from his right coat pocket and showed me the switchblade it held. As he pushed the button to open it, I could hear my heart pounding in my ears. My eyebrows were having a tough time coping with the sweat that was running down my forehead toward my eyes. I wanted so much to rub them to stop the stinging. Somehow, though, I didn't think I'd feel the sting of sweat, or anything else, for very much longer. I was about to die. Of that I was certain.

"I will ask you just one more time, Ian. Why are you in Moscow?"

I knew what was coming. I tensed my entire body as I answered. "I just told you, dipshit."

He plunged the knife into my left wrist. My scream echoed off the filthy, damp brick walls for what seemed an eternity. I stared down at my wrist as he pulled the blade out. Every time my heart would beat, blood would squirt out of the wound. At least it took my mind off the sweat getting into my eyes. Every knife does indeed have a silver edge.

The man was a total psychopath. I could see saliva forming

in the corners of his mouth. The bastard was going to start drooling in a second.

"It does not matter what you tell me, Ian. But before I let you bleed to death, I want you to know how stupid you are. Are you listening to me, Ian?"

He slapped me hard across the face to make sure he had my attention. "We are aware of everything you and that bitch, Irena Ryumin, have been doing. Everything."

My heart sank with the sound of her name. I no longer feared for my own safety. My every fiber was now concerned with Irena's well-being. Maybe she had time to get away. Maybe I was all he had.

"You think perhaps, Ian, that we don't have the slut traitor?"

It was as if he were reading my mind.

He motioned to the two GRU guards, who went through the door he had come out of. Seconds later they came back into the room with Irena between them.

She had her mouth taped closed and her hands were tied behind her back. Ivanchenko grabbed her by her beautiful blond hair and threw her to the dirty stone floor in front of me. When she looked up at me, our eyes locked.

"I love you, Irena," I whispered.

Her eyes held mine, and I could see her try to smile beneath the tape. She just nodded her head and fell against my legs.

Ivanchenko looked at his men. "How touching. Look how the traitorous woman clings to the American spy."

He again grabbed her by the hair and dragged her away from me. He then stared at me as he unbuttoned his coat. He kept staring. He would not blink. His right hand reached in under his left arm and came out with a pistol. "Ian. Let me show you how we deal with traitors in my country."

I screamed with pain as I tried to tear myself free from the chair. He leaned down, put the barrel of the gun against her temple, and pulled the trigger. Her body jerked and then lay still. Her light blue pants became stained as her muscles relaxed in death. Just like that, it was over.

But even as life left her, she looked so beautiful. So vibrant. I had to blink away the tears to get a good look at her. As she lay there on the cold, damp stone floor, with bright red blood pooling around her face, I thought of her skating on the ice at the sports center. That is where she should be now. That is where she belonged. Skating on the ice. Instead, she lay dead at my feet, because she fell in love with the wrong person. A person who had used her. A person who in a sense had just helped this heartless madman pull the trigger.

I started losing touch. The loss of blood and shock caused me to vomit. It was the last thing I remembered doing in that ugly, horrid chamber.

I woke up the next day at the American embassy. My left wrist was bandaged, as was my face. I felt like one of the undead.

The station chief was sitting next to my bed. "I'm sorry, Ian. You were thrown out of a car at two a.m. in front of the embassy. The whole thing is blown. I don't know how they got on to Irena. She must have tipped them off somehow."

Tipped them off. Sounds so simple. So clinical. I just stared down at the yellow blanket that covered my legs.

"Ian, the Soviets have given you forty-eight hours to leave

the country. You are persona non grata. They are expelling you for espionage. We're shipping you out of Sheremetyevo Airport on a nine a.m. flight back to New York."

Yes, I remember you well, Colonel Vladimir Ivanchenko. Welcome to my turf, my timing, and my justice. Welcome to the last city you will ever know.

15

So much for my trip down memory lane. Some people I know, that's all they do is stroll down that particularly unthreatening street. Personally, I think it's mostly a waste of time. I liked the present. Just where I was. In my little overpriced house in Dedham, Massachusetts, where unfortunately, I wasn't able to click my mind off and fall asleep until around 7:30 in the morning.

Less than two hours later the phone rang. When the machine didn't answer after the eighth ring, I figured it wasn't going to stop, so I picked up a Michael Crichton paperback off my nightstand and flung it at the phone. Missed it by a mile, but caught the lamp dead center.

I stumbled over and picked up the receiver. "Hello."

As I listened, I tried to pry my left eye open. It had become glued shut during my nap by sleep. As I pulled a long, gumlike strand of goo from my eyelid, I heard the voice of my secretary on the phone.

"Yes, Mrs. Casey. I know I left you a note to call me. No, I'm not grouchy. Yes, I know there is something sticky all over my desk. It's Pepsi. No, I didn't spill it."

I held the receiver away from my ear. The woman's voice was a natural bullhorn.

"No, I am not a slob, Mrs. Casey. I'm the 'Wallace' in Wallace Investigations, in case you want to remember that. What? No, I'm not threatening to fire you. Mrs. . . . Mrs. . . . Mrs. . . . Casey, please stop crying. You're right. I am a slob. A terrible slob. I'll try and be more neat."

Unbelievable. The grief I had to go through just to ask her to do something for me. No assistant in the world is worth this kind of trouble—even if she could type ninety-five words a minute and cover my ass at all times. If I hadn't been such a coward, and if I didn't love her because she *did* treat me that way, I *would* have fired her.

"Mrs. Casey? Diane? Are you listening to me? Have you stopped hyperventilating? Fine. Do you think you could do something for me?"

While she was thinking about it, I went over to the lamp. I pushed it with my toe just to make sure it wasn't faking. Nope. Dead as a doornail. I wondered if there was a bounty on this one?

"Complicated? No, this is very simple, Mrs. Casey. I just want you to call MIT and get the whereabouts of Professor Georgy Barkagan. No, not Groggy. Georgy. Just find out all you can about the guy and call me back, okay? No, I'm not mad at you. Bye."

I hung up and went into the bathroom to transfer some liquid. Once done, I washed my face, brushed my teeth with the Snoopy toothbrush my sister had given me, and went out to my kitchen in search of anything that might resemble a breakfast food.

I opened my refrigerator door and just as quickly closed it. It looked as if a cast party from *Night of the Living Dead* was taking place inside. Yuk. I *really* needed to learn to clean up after myself.

Walking back into my bedroom, I pulled on a golf shirt, stuck my feet in my almost permanently unlaced sneakers, hopped in my car, drove down the street to the Stop & Shop, and grabbed a copy of the *Boston Herald*, along with a package of whole-wheat English muffins and a quart of orange juice. The all-Anglo breakfast.

Once back home, I sat down at my kitchen table with the paper. Instead of reading, however, I found myself contemplating me for a moment.

The cruelties and happenstance of life aside, I had evolved into a fairly simple man. Any of my Boston sports teams on a winning streak, a still-to-be-finished good book by my side, an exceptional cup of coffee throwing off wafts of steam on the table before me, and at least the fantasy of a truly stunning, intelligent, and accomplished woman walking into my life who would think my various flaws are what made me at least partially attractive to her, and I'm a very happy human being.

After that random thought, I began staring at my kitchen table. Well, it's not really a table at all. It's kind of a kitchen bar that extends six feet from the wall and divides the kitchen from the dining room.

I have covered it with black granite and have built cabinets underneath it. They are walnut in color and substance and very sturdy.

I like to work with my hands. I'm never going to get to host a show on the Home & Garden network, but I do find it very relaxing. Puttering around the house is fun. My current project is turning my all too bland basement into a family room for my nonexistent wife, kids, and puppy.

Family room is also something of a misnomer. What I really want to do is turn it into the last bastion of American masculinity. I'm talking combination pool table/Ping-Pong table, plus a poker table, dartboard, bar, iPod sound system, LCD high-definition TV, and sofa bed.

Not that I am some kind of male chauvinist pig. Because I'm most certainly not. I am as far removed from the typical male as you can get. And to prove to myself how *untypical* I was, I immediately turned to the sports page. I used to read the paper normally, front to back, but all that bad news and the liberal bias pushed by most mainstream papers was starting to have a cumulative effect on my already fragile mind. So, to protect myself, I turned to the relative safety of the sports section. Mistake.

The headline YANKEES SWEEP SOX FOUR STRAIGHT assaults my eyeballs first and my inner sanctum second. I'm so depressed. I know it's wrong. Every year I say to myself, "Ignore the Red Sox. Forget 'em. Pretend they don't even exist." And every year I disobey myself. Even though the city has enjoyed sports success of late, in fact, with the Bruins' latest Stanley Cup title one could argue that we were the new Title Town, USA, I sometimes wonder if, overall, being a Boston sports fan is in reality some kind of purgatory on earth.

As an adult, I've morphed into a Christian who is not fond of organized religion, and one who believes that the ultimate sin and obscenity in life is to kill or hurt one of God's children in His name or in the name of a religion. As such, I tend not to pay much attention to the rules, scenarios, or warnings issued by the often hypocritical religious "leaders" of our time.

That said, as a child borderline raised in the Catholic faith, I knew purgatory was a threatened holding tank for those not quite ready for heaven. Its residents were sinners who, while apparently living selfish and hurtful lifestyles—politicians, teacher-union leaders, and network executives coming to mind—had not committed any unforgivable mortal sins.

As one of those parochial school students, I was never well liked by the nuns or the priests. My only sin, as far as I could tell, was having an inquisitive mind. "Never question the Church!" I was told time and time again. Little did they know that I considered it my job to question every adult incessantly and had most likely set the *Guinness Book of Records* mark for asking, "Why?"

In response to my repeated questions about the church or the faith, I was usually just told to go away and keep my logical but troublesome inquiries to myself. This by the same institution, mind you, that for centuries had St. George on its honor roll of saints.

And of course, we all know what good old George did for a living. He only killed dragons. Dragons. I guess it finally became too much for even the pope to keep a straight face over that one. So "line-through-name," you're history, George. Your sainthood has been permanently revoked.

Life is nothing if not ironic. As an adult, my line of work necessitated the killing of dragons. Since its beginning, the nation has asked the Central Intelligence Agency to fight dragons, mythical and otherwise. However, anytime members of Congress or a president needed a fall guy for mistakes of their making, "poof," the CIA has been magically and immediately consigned to the slag heap next to St. George. As evidence, look no further than the disaster that became Iraq or any public terrorism attempts or attacks. To paraphrase the movie *Ghostbusters*, "Who ya gonna blame? The CIA."

One person's faith or calling was another person's problem. On second thought, maybe George really did kill dragons and had just needed a better lawyer and public relations consultant.

Three decades later, my faith in the church has lapsed, and faith in the sanity of my government is shaky at best. For all that, however, I'm still more than willing to step into the breach to fight the metaphorical dragons. Why?

My basic reasoning for this has always been that people need to become engaged. More and more, as the world spirals out of control toward complete anarchy, human nature tells us not to get involved. No matter what the problem is, ignore it, walk away, and hope someone else will deal with it. Therein lies a major reason for the slow destruction of our nation and of humanity. In general, almost no one is going to get involved. No one is willing to fight dragons.

See a parent abusing a child in public. Walk away. See a young and frightened girl walk into an abortion clinic to end a precious and sacred life. Say nothing. See three lowlifes terrorizing riders on the subway, close your eyes and hope they don't pick on you. See someone leave a backpack behind in a mall. Run from the mall and never tell anyone. Dragons come in all shapes and sizes. Some beat their wives, some assassinate world leaders, and some are all too willing to detonate a nuclear weapon in the name of "God."

All dragons. And all have to be slayed in one way or another. For better or worse, that's what I do, and that's what I'll always do. I can't walk away. I can't close my eyes and I can't ignore the problem. I confront the dragons, hope I'm right, and hope I survive the experience. With each battle, the odds grow against me and those who share my beliefs.

16

---

ooking back down at the *Boston Herald*, I started reading how all of the Red Sox problems would be solved if only they could get some pitching. Where have I heard that one before? Enough fiction for one morning. I decided to head over to the local baseball field and run off the breakfast I had just ingested.

It was eleven o'clock in the morning. It was 72 degrees, a cloudless blue sky, and school vacation had just begun. Do you think there'd be a kid to be found anywhere on the baseball field? Not a chance. Nobody. I had the place to myself.

What happened to every little boy's dream of growing up to be a major-league baseball player? Where's the practice? The dedication to perfection? The drive to succeed? I'll tell you where. It's taken up residence in the poor little boys of the Dominican Republic, Haiti, and Venezuela. Here in the United States, the dream is atrophying in front of a TV eating junk food and playing the latest Xbox or PlayStation games.

As I pounded out my three miles in the bright sunshine, I castigated myself for forgetting my iPod mini. I'm with the kids on that one. I love listening to tunes as I fight to stay in shape. I just prefer to listen while in motion and not parked on a sofa.

I finished my run in just over twenty minutes and started my slow walk back to my house. I have exercised regularly since I was sixteen. I believe in it. The old expression that states "Your body is your temple" has a lot of merit. It makes me feel good to work out, and it keeps the pounds off. It gives me more energy at the end of a long day, and it makes my mind seem that much sharper. Which in my case is asking a lot.

Until the day comes that I cough up a lung, I will always make some kind of attempt at giving my 196 pounds of flesh and bones some kind of workout. Plus, as shallow as it may sound, I like the woman I'm with to be physically attractive and in shape, and so I feel that it is only fair that I reciprocate in kind.

The phone was ringing as I entered my front door. I threw my keys on the sofa, jogged into the kitchen, and picked it up.

"Hello, Mrs. Casey."

Surprise, surprise. It wasn't Mrs. Casey. It was one of Phil's friends from the Agency. One of his *female* friends. Her voice sounded as if, in her spare time, she practiced writhing nude on a bearskin rug in front of a roaring fireplace, just waiting for you to get home.

She said she had just flown in from D.C. and needed to meet with me as soon as possible. Phil didn't believe in wasting time. I told her I would meet her in one hour in front of the old Dedham Square movie theater, gave her directions, and hung up. One hour. Just enough time to take a quick shower and to make myself look somewhat presentable.

As I hurried toward the shower, I thought, Hey, wait a minute. Experience has taught all of us that voices like that very rarely match up physically. So what's the rush? On the other hand, I knew Phil very well. I knew how his sick little mind worked. It would be just like him to supply me with an incentive to keep me interested in the assignment.

I got to the movie theater twenty minutes early and decided to grab a Pepsi at the sandwich shop next store. After waiting ten minutes for the high school girl on her cell phone to take my order, I finally got my Pepsi and sat at a table facing the street. No sooner did I take my first sip than the CIA woman's taxi pulled up in front of the theater.

As she stepped out of the cab, my heart did a quadruple reverse, with two and a half twists. Degree of difficulty 3.8. I was in trouble. Big trouble. The woman was stunning. As the saying goes, "She had the kind of body that would make a straight bishop kick a hole through a stained glass window." The kind of body that would make the rest of us mere mortal males go beat our heads senseless against a tree stump, somewhere deep in the enchanted forest. Where in the world was she when I was with the Agency? I always got to work with the Miss Hathaway look-alikes from *The Beverly Hillbillies*.

She pulled a small black suitcase out of the cab, paid the driver, and just stood there looking very goddess-like. As she looked down to check her iPhone, one guy turned to admire her and walked right into a parking meter. Ouch. She had thick black hair that was cut into some kind of very expensive-looking shape. Her eyes were a mystery, hidden behind a pair of red-trimmed sunglasses. And she had the best tan I had ever seen.

I mean, Coppertone would be afraid to use her because of claims of false advertising on their part. Deep, dark, dangerous.

She wore a red button-down short-sleeve shirt. The top

three buttons were undone to highlight what looked to me to be bigger-than-average breasts. Her slacks were jet black and clung to every part of her lower body. She had on black high heel shoes, and a black Coach purse was slung over her right shoulder.

She also had a gold chain around her neck with a small gold cross at the bottom. The cross, reflected in the early afternoon sunlight, could have conveyed any number of unspoken messages.

If I worked in a carnival, I would have guessed she was five feet, seven inches tall and weighed in around 125 pounds. In my haste to get out to meet her, I spilled some Pepsi onto my pants. Normally that wouldn't be such a terrible thing, but this afternoon I had decided to wear my cream-colored khakis and a dark blue golf shirt.

Needless to say, the more I rubbed the stain, the worse it looked. In fact all my effort had turned it into what looked very much like an arrow, pointing toward my zipper. Want a piece of candy, little girl? The hell with it, I thought. There was nothing I could do now except walk out and accept the inevitable.

When I did walk out the door and started to move toward her, I saw her head immediately look down at my stain. She then looked up at my face and giggled. Swell. I just hoped that she wasn't one of those people who base their *entire* opinion of you on their first impression.

As I got closer, she looked to be in the thirty to thirty-five-year-old range. However, I must confess that my ability to guess a woman's age is a joke. I have honestly found myself admiring what I considered to be women, only to be told later that these "women" were all of sixteen. In my own defense, I defy anyone to guess the age of some of these teenage girls. I know I can't.

I walked up to her and extended my hand. "Kathy Donahue, I presume."

She took off her shades and shook my hand. Brown eyes so dark they were almost a coal black. Better and better.

"And you must be Ian." She looked down at my pants and back up at me. "Is that the latest style from Armani?"

I'm kind of ashamed to admit it, but having reached middle age, I still have a tendency to blush like a teenager asked to dance at his first boy/girl social. I felt my ears warming up as I turned my body sideways. I reached down and picked up her suitcase.

"Come on. My car's just across the street."

And so it was. My black, pre-owned Jaguar S-Type was still there. Not always a sure bet when you live next to Boston, the stolen car capital of the world.

The Jaguar was easily the most extravagant thing I owned. Being that I'm in the private detective and bodyguard business, I've had more than a few friends and clients kid me about the car because it's "British," and so is James Bond. The fact that I bought it used from a little old lady living next door to me who was moving to Florida did not seem to get me off the hook. They simply decided I was a James Bond wannabe. Regardless, when the car worked right, it was a powerful, effective, and impressive machine.

As she was getting in, I said, "Well, look at that. I just met you, and already we have something in common."

She shook her head a little, as if she were just getting ready to hear another of the many lines thrown her way by men on the make. "And what might that be?"

"Black."

"Pardon me?"

"Black. Your pants are black and so is my car."

"My, that is a coincidence. I bet the odds on that are positively minuscule."

Her looks and attitude were throwing me off kilter. A line that lame was what you'd expect to come out of the mouth of the pre-puber I'd suddenly reverted to. As we were driving, though, it was on to more serious business.

"No offense, Kathy. But can I see some kind of ID?"

As she reached in her purse, I caught sight of a Bersa Thunder 380 pistol. Nice touch. Just don't blow off my kneecap by accident while you're playing around in there.

She didn't, and the ID checked out just fine.

I nodded down at the purse. "What's the hardware for?"

She instinctively touched her bag as I asked the question.

"Oh, nothing special. My mother warned me about the men from Boston, so I just thought I'd come prepared."

After five more minutes of small talk, I pulled into my driveway and put it into park.

"To your point about men from Boston. Not to worry. As a matter of fact, the only guys I'd watch out for, if I were you, are the ones who always have their shirt collars turned up like Elvis and drink designer water while they drive their Benzes to the club for a game of squash."

She laughed. "Really?"

"Yeah, but don't worry too much. You usually need a crowbar to pry them away from their mirrors, country clubs, and investment portfolios."

"Yikes. Where did that come from?"

"Dorchester," I smiled. "Enough said."

We went into the house and I showed her where the bathroom was so she could freshen up. While she was doing that, I went to my room to change into a pair of black khakis. When we both came out, I asked her if I could get her anything to drink.

"I'll have a cup of tea, if you have any."

"As a matter of fact, I do. Someone I used to know loved the stuff. So I got in the habit of keeping some around."

Kathy sat down on the arm of my white sofa. "Someone you *used* to know?"

I filled the copper kettle with water and put it on to boil.

"Yeah. It was a lifetime ago."

"Moscow?"

It was obvious—and expected—that Kathy would have been briefed about Irena and my past Agency life before showing up. More stupid and useless games.

I frowned and bit my lower lip. "Look, why don't we dispense with this bit of small talk if you don't mind."

Her smile became more artificial as she cranked it up a few watts. "No, I don't mind at all. We can talk about the weather or who you took to your high school prom instead."

I grabbed a couple of Mikasa blue and white cups out of the cupboard and put them on the counter as the kettle whistled at us. I filled the cups with boiling water and set them on the bar, placed the milk and sugar between us, and sat back down.

We now had to wait for our tea to steep. As we did, the silence officially became awkward.

I didn't care. Let it get awkward. She should not have gone there.

As she continued to bite her tongue, Kathy kept staring into my eyes from across the bar. It felt as if someone had hit me in the face with a lead pipe. Not a good sign.

"You still love her, don't you?"

So much for the weather, my high school prom, or will-power, for that matter.

I paused and slowly shook my head before finally answering. "I miss her . . . and I sometimes wonder what . . ."

I stopped instantly as I felt the lump in my throat. I looked back into Kathy's eyes and saw the recognition that she knew exactly what I sometimes wondered about. My unborn child.

"Shit," I barked out as I walked to the center of my kitchen.

Two seconds after I said it, I realized I had sworn. I know it sounds kind of old-fashioned, but I don't like to swear in front of women. I still pull out chairs for them, and I still open car doors for them. Equal rights or not. I would feel wrong if I didn't do those things.

"Sorry about the language," I mumbled.

She stood, walked over, and touched the back of my hand. It felt as if the ground had shifted under my feet.

"Don't worry about it," she said. "I'm the one who needs to apologize for prying. I know better than that."

I nodded at her now genuine smile. "Noted and accepted. I have to make a quick call to my office and then we'll be off."

She looked amused as I placed the call. Her wheels were spinning, and I had no idea in what direction.

"Hi, Mrs. Casey."

Kathy picked up her teacup and walked over to look out the kitchen window. As she did, I turned to admire her and the fit of her black Donna Karan slacks.

"I'm sorry, Mrs. Casey. I didn't expect you to call back that soon. Where was I? Well, if you really need to know to get on with the rest of your life, I was out running. Now can you just give me what you have on the professor?"

She did, and I started writing it all down on the back of my electric bill. I always meant to get one of those cute little message boards that you stick up next to the phone. But I never quite got around to it. One of my many flaws is procrastination. In lighter moments, my mantra is, If something were worth doing, it would have been done already.

"You're a diamond in the rough, Diane," I said as I hung up.

Kathy raised her eyebrows. "Diane?"

I folded the paper and stuck it in my front pants pocket.

"Yeah, Diane. My assistant. She's about sixty years old. Really upsets her every time I call her that. Thinks I should call her Mrs. or Ms. Casey. She is a very proper Brit from London whom I, in fact, love very much. Truth be told, she keeps my business and my office from turning into a smoking black crater in the ground."

Just then the phone rang again. Kathy arched her dark eyebrows at me but said nothing.

"Hello," I said in the middle of the second ring.

"Who's your buddy? Who's your pal?" asked a male voice.

I looked over at Kathy and into the phone said, "Hi, Phil."

"Tell me," he laughed, "that she's not the most smoking-hot government employee you've ever seen."

I nodded my head into the phone. "No argument from me on that score."

I could hear Phil's chair squeak as I guessed he leaned back. "Yeah, well, don't let that beauty cloud your pea brain. She did over a year in Afghanistan and saw and did some serious shit. She's tough, she's professional, and she'll watch your back. You can trust her."

I paused a second, thought about Ivanchenko, and said, "I doubt it," and hung up.

Kathy walked toward me. "What do you doubt?"

I started for the front door and laughed. "Anything Phil says. Now, let's head out, ma'am. We're burning daylight," I said in my best John Wayne imitation.

She didn't believe me about Phil, but was polite enough not to call me a liar as we headed out the door.

17

I took Route 128 to Route 3 into Boston. Route 1 is a straight shot, but the traffic lights will drive you to drink. The word around the country is that if you can drive in Boston, then you can drive anywhere. I know every city says that about itself, but I have actually seen articles on Boston drivers in several cities around the country. One such big-city newspaper stated that Boston drivers were the absolute worst in the world. That article just happened to be in the ultraliberal *New York Times*. The paper of record for the city all true Bostonians hate.

Hate may be too strong a word. That said, the "intense dislike" all stems from the Red Sox–Yankees rivalry. Rivalry or not, one thing the *New York Times* is right about is our driving. We have to be the worst.

You can take the meekest, mildest man or woman in Boston and stick him behind the wheel of a car, and in seconds you've got yourself a road-rage serial killer. There is something about traffic and a car that catapults most Bostonians right back to the Dark Ages. I claim no immunity from this disease. I can froth at the mouth as well as the next guy when someone cuts me off at rush hour. Amped-up testosterone on a silver platter.

Once, while driving with my cousin down in Maryland,

some local redneck in a pickup truck almost drove us off the road. When we caught up to him at the next light, I jumped out of our car and tried to drag him from his truck through the side window. Luckily, my cousin was smart enough to pull me off him before the state police arrived and decided to put a few rounds into the back of my head for practice. I'm told that the cops in the South get bonus pay if they ring up a Yankee.

Kathy and I were driving down 128 south at just under sixty-five miles per hour. "Just under" is very important. For as long as you keep it under that magic number, the local police will pretty much leave you alone. Most of their radar guns beep at sixty-five and above.

I turned to look at her. "I thought the Agency was going to stay on the sidelines on this one?"

"We are," she answered as she examined the red nail polish on the fingers of her right hand.

"So what are you here for, then?" I asked as the engine of the Jag begged to go eighty.

She reached into her purse and came out with a Newport cigarette, which she promptly fired up. As she did, I grunted.

"Oh, I'm sorry. Do you mind if I smoke?"

I grunted again, and looked over at the white smoke escaping both her nose and mouth as it drifted toward her partly open window.

"Aren't people supposed to ask first, then start smoking?"

"You're right. I guess you want me to put it out."

"Normally I would. But in your case I'll make an exception."

She shook her head and her thick black hair moved and then fell back into its expensive cut. "Nope. A rule is a rule. I shall respect your wishes. This is, after all, your car."

She pitched the cigarette out the window. I only caught a

quick glimpse of it in the rearview mirror. But to me it looked like it landed right in the middle of an old pile of dry leaves, next to the forest.

"So why are you here?" I asked again.

"Well, to tell you the truth, I'm just dying to watch a big, strong private eye at work. I mean I get goose bumps all over just thinking about it."

Strange. The sentence started off light enough. But toward the end there, she started sounding very sarcastic. I could see Phil's fine hand in this.

"What's with the sarcasm?"

She stared back down at her fingernails, like a little kid does when you're asking them how the plate got broken. A very attractive quality, in my humble opinion. The little girl in the woman, that is. Not the fingernails.

She pursed her lips and said, "I just don't understand why you left the Agency for this line of work."

She said "this line of work" as if she were saying, "You mean, you actually *eat* the worms?" Clearly, not on her top-ten list of career positions.

There was a large, gas-guzzling SUV just in front of my car. In the back were three little girls looking out at us. Sisters, I assumed. The oldest looked to be about twelve, and the youngest about seven. Three very cute little redheads with freckles. I waved at the youngest one and offered up a weak smile.

She stuck here tongue out at me and flashed me the finger. Another MTV disciple. Ya gotta watch out for those redheads. A lesson I had learned all too well in the past.

"Look, Kathy," I said. "As you made clear back at my house, you read my file before you ever set foot in Boston. So why don't we give each other the courtesy of honesty. You know as well as I do why I left the Agency. As to why I'm in this line of work, well, the answer is simplicity itself. I enjoy helping people. It gives me a purpose. As strange as it may sound, there are still people in this world who like to do things like that. You happen to be sitting next to one right now."

We were driving past the giant gas tank at Neponset Circle, painted by that nun a long time ago. They say that if you look at the blue paint pattern on the gas tank, you can see the profile of Ho Chi Minh, the late communist leader of North Vietnam. Something, I'm sure, that pleases Vietnam vets to no end. Drive around your hometown of Boston and see the face of some shit-kicking little dictator from a former bamboo empire staring down at you. And people wonder why Vietnam vets still feel just a tad bit put-upon?

Kathy was quiet for several minutes before she said, "I'm sorry."

I beeped at the kids in the SUV as their father took an off-ramp. Creeps.

"No. Don't apologize," I said.

That seemed to trip her up.

"Pardon me?"

I smiled at her. "I mean it. It's one of the rules I lived by. Never apologize for saying something you truly mean. It will only tend to compromise you and your integrity. If you said it, then stick with it. It won't make you too popular with your friends, but they should respect you for it."

It sounded good, but she wasn't buying it.

"What a crock of shit that is."

We were coming up to the Mass Avenue bridge leading into Cambridge. "Does your mother know that you talk like that?

You know, when men swear, it's usually to make themselves sound more macho. What's your excuse?"

"I can't believe it," she said. "You're really serious. You think it's wrong for women to swear, don't you? That it somehow makes us less feminine."

"Yup."

She had replaced her happy face with a frown. "Wow. I thought men like you went out with the chastity belt."

I pushed a button on my steering wheel and lowered the volume on the classical station currently playing Mozart. "Nah. We're staging a comeback. There's more and more of us crawling out from under that rock I escaped from."

She laughed. I was growing to love that sound. "You're making fun of me," she said.

"Well, maybe just a little bit. Now, for the final time, why are you here?"

She started running a yellow plastic brush through her hair as we approached MIT. "One," she said, "to keep an eye on you. And two, to bring you your money as well as a little extra for, ah, unforeseen expenses."

Now she had my interest. "Speaking of which, where is it?"

Out next came the red lip gloss. "Back at your house, in my suitcase."

That didn't make me feel too secure. Hadn't she ever heard of burglars and the ever increasing crime problem?

"It's all in cash, I presume," I said.

"What else?"

What else indeed. I remember the first time I had to deal with the CIA in terms of money. It was after my physical and polygraph and whatnot. I went to a room at headquarters to be reimbursed for my plane fare and other expenses. I figured that they would write me a check for my expenses and that would be that. Not so. I sat down with an absolute doll named Patty, who liked showing off her considerable cleavage.

Patty asked me what my expenses were, and I told her. I waited for her to write out the check, but it never happened. Instead she pulled open a desk drawer and my eyes almost fell out of my head. There must have been over ten thousand dollars in cash sitting there. She counted out my money, and asked me in a cute little voice, "Are you sure there aren't any more expenses we could pay for? It's okay if you can't find the receipts. Really, it is."

I knew it! I thought. The final test to see who was dirtbag enough to cheat on their expenses? Well not me, sister. I'm not blowing my career over a couple of hundred bucks. Of course, years later, I found out it wasn't a test at all, and that the money was mine for the taking. Patty, as I found out later, just liked young and in-shape men . . . a lot.

As we walked up to the sprawling university, I thought about how strange MIT really was, and how fitting it was that it should be located in Cambridge. I think of myself as being a fairly conservative person. I'm not exactly three goose steps to the right of Genghis Khan, but I'm out there.

While I may have been conservative in certain things, I was in no way political. When I was in the field and my ass was on the line, it quickly dawned on me that the vast majority of politicians, regardless of political persuasion, cared about my sacrifice, the sacrifice of my colleagues, or the sacrifice of our troops only if they could somehow exploit it for their own selfish needs. Both parties made my skin crawl on a regular basis.

Republicans who never served in the military—and in fact

actively and creatively avoided it—would disgustingly question the patriotism of Democrats, amazingly, even those who served heroically in our armed services.

Wealthy Democratic members and staffers who wore their outright disdain for the military on their sleeves and gleefully referred to a three-star general grievously wounded in combat as a "warmonger" were just as repulsive as the chicken-hawk Republican eggheads calling for more and more young Americans to be sent into harm's way to satisfy their pet ivory tower academic theories.

In the world of today, where Muslim extremists plan their next massive attack against us, too many Republicans and Democrats still choose to put self and party before country. Fanatics on either side of the political spectrum cause me great concern.

That is why I always get a somewhat queasy feeling whenever I enter Cambridge. It is an exceptionally liberal city. Lots of fanatics. I think the latest poll I saw in the *Boston Herald* stated that almost 75 percent of the inhabitants considered themselves to be *very* liberal. Seventy-five percent. I don't think Beijing comes close to that number. The only places on earth that might be more liberal than Cambridge are our own State Department and the United Nations.

The fanatically liberal people who live in Cambridge honestly align themselves more with the inhuman socialist agendas of North Korea and Venezuela than with what is happening in their own town. It still seems to be a haven for overage hippies who always need some cause to believe in. Something to protest. Because if they did not have something to rail against, then they'd have to take a good long, hard look at themselves in a mirror and realize that they have grown old and life is passing them by. That they are protesting life rather than living it. The kind of people who insisted on saying "Happy holidays" at Christmas and were offended or thought you a bigot for saying the perfectly proper "Merry Christmas" in a nation that was more than 80 percent Christian.

Like Harvard, the Massachusetts Institute of Technology fits into Cambridge like a hand in a glove. Perfect. The faculty and student population are so far left as to make Mao and Lenin smile up in pride from hell.

As one who had worked with Mossad and the Israel Defense Forces in the past, remained a very strong supporter of the state of Israel, and had many friends in the country, I always became particularly incensed whenever I saw one of these spoiled, rich, never-had-to-serve-their-nation liberal brats walk past me wearing a keffiyeh scarf in "solidarity with the Palestinian people." The same "populist" idiots who wear the Che Guevara T-shirts and have no idea of the atrocities that man committed against homosexuals, blacks, women, and children.

I've seen and experienced enough suffering to last several lifetimes, and I truly want peace for the Israeli and Palestinian peoples. Enough is enough. That said, idiotic political fashion statements by ignorant trust-fund babies who don't know the difference between a democracy and dictatorship, or a country where women have freedom and equality and one where women are second-class citizens or often much worse, are beyond the pale. Grow up.

It was a strange university and a stranger city. Fortunately, we did not have to stay long.

A quick visit to the school revealed that Dr. Barkagan was nowhere to be found. He was instead doing his research work at MIT's Lincoln Laboratory in Lexington, Massachusetts. Wonderful. Maybe this wild-goose chase was Mrs. Casey's way of punishing me.

In the meantime, it was off to Lincoln Lab to meet with the elusive Ph.D. A quick phone call confirmed that he was in fact there and that he would stay put until our arrival.

18

As we walked back to my car, Kathy tugged on the back of my shirt and whispered, "Shadows at six o'clock."

I pushed a button on my key chain to unlock the doors of the Jaguar and opened the passenger door for Kathy. As I waited for her to get in, I swiveled my head slightly toward the back of the car and took a quick peek.

Sure enough, three cars back were two very Slavic-looking gentlemen trying hard to be inconspicuous.

After closing Kathy's door, I walked around behind the car, took another look at the two goons, and got in the driver's side.

"Nice eyesight, Mr. Magoo." I smiled at Kathy as I buckled my seat belt.

Kathy flipped down the visor above her head and pretended to fix her hair while using the mirror to keep an eye on our new friends.

"They can't be here for us," she said as she wiped a bit of lipstick off her teeth.

I turned the key in the ignition and started the car. "Nope. They're doing the same thing we are. Looking for Barkagan."

Kathy reached into her purse and clicked the safety off on her pistol. "Uh-oh," she said, looking back into the mirror.

"What?" I asked, not seeing anything in my side-view mirror.

"One of the Ivans is on his cell phone."

I glanced at my side mirror again and pulled out into the street. "Getting instructions from Mommy."

Fifty feet down the street, I looked up at my rearview mirror and saw the black Crown Victoria with the two Ivans pull out and start to follow us.

"I guess they've been told to make new friends," I said as I applied more pressure to the accelerator.

My guess was the Ivans had been told to follow us to see if we would lead them to Barkagan. Wrong. We were not one hundred yards down the street when the Crown Vic tried to pull up next to us while doing about forty miles per hour.

It's amazing how many times I've been wrong in my life. If I were a baseball player, I wouldn't even be batting my weight.

I turned my head left just in time to see the shotgun barrel poking out the passenger window of the Ford.

I slammed on the very good brakes of the Jaguar a millisecond before seeing the flash from the muzzle of the shotgun and hearing the deafening blast. The Crown Vic accelerated down the street with the shooter most likely not realizing that the blast had missed us completely.

I turned to check on Kathy, but she was no longer in the passenger seat. Before I could fully comprehend what was happening, I heard a number of loud gunshots. I looked up at the rapidly receding car and saw its rear window shatter. Just as quickly, Kathy jumped back into the car with a hint of white smoke wafting from the barrel of her Bersa. Maybe a new pope had just been elected.

In a matter of a few seconds, Kathy ejected the spent clip, slammed in a new one, clicked on the safety, threw the gun in her purse, and looked over at me.

"Whatever we're paying you," she said as she flipped the visor down again and fixed her hair, "is not enough."

I stepped on the gas before one of the Bolsheviks in Cambridge could get a read on my plate and report me to the "Oppressive Pigs."

"Yeah." I nodded. "I'll take that up with Phil at our next shareholders meeting. In the meantime, we'd better reach Barkagan before those guys."

Kathy smiled over at me. "Ya think?"

I quietly nodded my head in response. Badass with a body. Maybe Phil was right about her being the complete package.

19

My first impression of Barkagan was that the man had to have been an extra in The Lord of the Rings. Troll-like and mean. The three of us sat at a small table in a Lincoln Lab cafeteria. I was drinking a Pepsi, Kathy was having a coffee, regular, and the troll was sipping a bottle of Evian water. Stuff that I have long suspected to be scooped out of French toilet bowls to be sold to gullible Americans.

It seemed that one of the many concessions our government had made to this clown was that he be supplied with a constant supply of Evian wherever and whenever he wanted. As I looked at him sitting across from me, I thought, *It figures.* Why couldn't he be like other past former Soviet defectors and ask for prostitutes to be supplied by the United States? No, this guy wants, and gets, water with an upscale label.

When I was with the Agency, we never trusted these "defectors." We always assumed that they were KGB plants. And we were usually right. What the KGB would do was take someone who had obvious value to the United States, like a KGB agent or a prominent scientist, and have him or her walk into the nearest U.S. embassy and request asylum. The KGB's goal in planting this person was really twofold. The obvious was to gather information. Any kind of information. Most Americans always had a number of misconceptions about the KGB. One of them was that they only went after "top-secret" information. And that was wrong. They went after everything and anything. Once collected, they brought the information back to the former Soviet Union and completed another piece of the jigsaw puzzle called "How to beat the United States intelligence apparatus."

One way they used to accomplish this was quite simple, yet highly effective. Once we got a defector, we brought him to a safe house and questioned him for months on end about different subjects to make sure that he was not a plant.

Now, if Boris was a plant, and he was on his toes, he might have been able to garner certain facts about the way the Agency operates by the pattern of our questions. Or he might be able to spread KGB disinformation and have us believe the lies. It happened. No matter how careful we were, we got burned from time to time.

The KGB's second goal in doing this was to embarrass the United States and, indirectly, the Central Intelligence Agency. The way they accomplished this was to have their "defector" walk away from his Agency escorts one day and back into a Soviet embassy, usually in Washington. Once that was done, the Soviets called a news conference and invited a worldwide media audience. As soon as the circus began, they trucked out their "defector," who proceeded to tell a very sad and terrorizing tale.

It seemed, in reality, that we bullies in the United States kidnapped this poor slob right off the street and subjected his poor little Marxist body to all kinds of elaborate tortures at Langley. He considered himself very fortunate indeed to have escaped with his life from his psychotic captors at the Agency.

And there you have it, public relations, KGB-style. World-wide headlines the next day. Even then, anti-Americanism was widespread in the foreign media, so the job of the KGB was made that much easier by European—and American—editors who were only too happy to ensure that the Politburo-manufactured mud stuck to our country and the Agency. The rest of the world was and is more than willing, even anxious, to believe the worst about the United States.

I have often wondered what would happen in this country if an agent from the CIA suddenly defected to North Korea. And with him went the blueprint designs for our latest "se-cret" weapon. How would the media react? I used to think they would label him the traitor that he was, but in the post-9/11 media environment we all live in, I'm no longer sure. Some edi-torial pages and networks in our country might now hail such a person as a "hero."

While he might be a hero to some in the media and some in the blogosphere who have never had to fight for their country for the privilege of criticizing it, for me and many I know a per-son like that would be a traitor and most definitely never to be trusted.

Such is the dilemma the Central Intelligence Agency has to deal with. Even if the defector is legit and really wants to stay in the United States, you can never fully trust him or her. In the intelligence business, the defector is a sleazebag. Of course, you'll never hear them called that in public. No, in public they will canonize him and state what a great human being he is for leaving the clutches of the Evil Empire for the safety and sanctuary of the good old U.S. of A.

In the minds of the CIA and FBI counterintelligence types, however, the defector is still only one thing: a traitor. And if he or she comes across with the goods, they will reward that person with their thirty pieces of silver, but will never ever trust them. They would be crazy if they did.

So right away I had a chip on my shoulder about Barkagan. But if he could deliver Ivanchenko to me, he'd be worth keeping alive. For the time being anyway.

In the car on the way over, Kathy and I decided it best not to mention our little live-fire exercise with the Russian Mafia. It was bad enough that our heart rates were still something over 150 beats per minute. No sense causing a full-blown panic attack in the professor.

As my mind stopped wandering, I suddenly realized that Barkagan was addressing me. Not pleasantly, either.

"I do not think I will be requiring a, how do you say, a baby-sitter, Mr. Wallace. I think I'm a very big boy now."

You may be a big boy now Ivan, I thought, but you're also an incredibly ugly boy. Geez, what an eyesore. Maybe Russia instituted a project to beautify the country and threw him out as part of the program. He looked like a bowling ball with skin. He stood about five feet four, and must have weighed over 250 pounds. He had thick black hair that seemed to fly out in a hundred different directions. Straight out of a session of electroshock therapy, and his must have run overtime.

He had two prominent warts on the left side of his face and yellow teeth. His face was shiny with oil, and his eyes protruded from his head. The man not only looked bad, but smelled like low tide in Boston Harbor. Hygiene was not his life calling. I noticed Kathy trying hard to position herself upwind of him, as her nose seemed to be trying to involuntarily close itself.

I had to remind myself to be diplomatic with this gentleman. I was, after all, unofficially a representative of the United States. Besides, I didn't want them taking back my money, or worse, taking away my human bait. I needed this greaseball to get to Ivanchenko.

"Professor Barkagan, I am just informing you of my government's concern for your safety. It would be very dangerous for you to refuse our offer of protection. The Russian Mafia is very dangerous and would very much like to get their hands on as much of your money as possible."

A slight understatement on my part. If Ivanchenko ever hooked his claws into this butterball, he was going to pound him into a meat grinder, body part by body part, and laugh every second while he churned way.

Sitting there, Barkagan reminded me of one of those perverts you see getting caught in a network sting operation. The reason that particular thought blossomed in my mind was the way he was staring at Kathy's chest.

He addressed me while still trying to see through Kathy's shirt. "I appreciate your government's concern, Mr. Wallace. But I can't afford to have you getting in my way while I complete my studies."

I leaned over and snapped my fingers in his face to get his attention away from Kathy. "Ahoy there, professor. I don't know about you, but my mother always taught me to look at the person I'm talking to. In this country, we call it manners."

Kathy sat forward in her chair. "Ian."

Barkagan didn't like it, either. "I think that is quite enough, thank you. I wish for you and Miss Donahue to please leave now."

I was pleased to note that this time Professor Barkagan was looking at *me*. Staring daggers, in fact. Fine by me, fat boy. When I was a kid I used to have staring contests with my cat. And the cat always left cross-eyed.

"I really don't think you're in a position to ask for much of anything right now, professor," I said. "As a matter of fact, for the next two weeks you only have one job. And that is to do exactly what I tell you to do. Understand?"

Instead of answering, he went over to a blue wall phone, picked it up, and said a few words. It didn't require a Rhodes scholar to figure out what was going to happen next. Thirty seconds later, two security guards hurried into the room.

The first was a black guy about thirty-five to forty years of age. He was about my size, and looked fairly tough. His nose had been broken at least once, and there was extensive scar tissue around his eyes. It was my general belief that he would require caution on my part. The other guard was a total waste of good worrying time. He was a toy cop. He wore a blue blazer decorated with some kind of security patch on the front. The first guy had to wear a regular old white short-sleeve shirt and black pants, but not this guy. He wore his blue blazer, gray slacks, white shirt, and blue tie, while carrying a walkie-talkie in his right hand. His "I'm the boss" ensemble.

Upon arrival, he spoke into the walkie-talkie. I couldn't hear what he said, but I'm sure it wasn't to tell the boys up in security to set two extra places for dinner.

He then walked up to Barkagan. "What seems to be the problem, professor?"

As he asked the question, he looked down at me and gave

me his hard-ass look. I ignored him and stole a quick glance at his backup. He seemed very relaxed, but I knew better. He was standing away from the table out of arm's reach, and had his body turned in a fighter's stance.

"The problem is, I want these two out of the building. They are bothering me," Barkagan said.

The guy in the blazer nodded his head, reached down, and grabbed me by the arm. "Okay, pal. You and the lady. Let's go."

Kathy reached across the table and held my wrist. "Ian, don't do anything. I can take care of this."

I looked up at the other security guard. "Listen, I'm about to dance a bit with your boss here. What are you going to do when I start?"

He gave me his best shark smile. "Well, no offense. But I'll be forced to get in your face some. I'm backing my paycheck."

Kathy jumped up and slammed the tabletop with her palm. Her blue cafeteria chair clattered to the black-and-white specked granite floor behind her. "Nobody," she said, "is getting in anyone's face, because *nothing* is going to happen!"

She shoved the Blazer's arm away from me, picked up her chair, and sat back down. The look on his face was worth the price of admission. She then turned her wrath on Professor Barkagan.

"Look, you ungrateful little bastard. If you don't do exactly what Mr. Wallace tells you to do, *when* he tells you, I'll have your fat ass deported back to Russia just as fast as they can process the paperwork. And in case you have any doubts as to my authority, I am speaking for my government on the issue. Do I make myself quite clear, professor?"

From where I was sitting, it seemed perfectly clear. The blood had drained from Barkagan's already pasty face. Making him look all the more repulsive. Something I thought impossible until that very moment.

"That is not possible. I am doing very important work for your country. You would not dare try such a thing."

She gave him a look the guy in the blazer only wished he could master. "Try me . . . *defector*."

Barkagan seemed to recoil from her aggressive tone. "I do not appreciate your words. You should try to treat me with more respect."

I took the opportunity to ease myself back into the conversation. "That is exactly our point, professor. You must try and treat *us* with more respect. Treat us as the professionals we are. Try and understand that we are only trying to save your life."

I gave him my "We're all buddies here" smile and continued: "It's really a very simple choice. Do what we ask, which is, after all, only in your best interest, or have these guys catch up with you, rip out your fingernails until you give them everything they want, put a bullet in the back of your head, and then dump your body in a shallow grave. The decision is of course yours to make, but unfortunately you must make it right this second."

All in all, it was one of the easier decisions Barkagan was ever going to have to make in his lifetime. And he knew it.

"Very well," he said. "I'll do what you ask."

I nodded at the Blazer. "Fine. Now why don't you tell Spider-Man here that he can go back to where he was and continue pulling on his limp dick."

That got a chuckle out of the other security guard, who seemed to be trying to figure out how well he would look in his boss's blazer.

I turned to him. "You ever do any boxing?"

He nodded his head slowly and showed me most of his teeth. "Yeah, I done me some."

"I thought so. Where?"

He turned both palms upward and shrugged his shoulders.

"Around. You know. But mostly up in Lowell. I did Golden Gloves up there for awhile."

"So why did you quit?"

Now I got to see all of his teeth. "'Cause I was a sucker for a left hook. I figured I best get out while I was still with the program. You know what I mean?"

Indeed I did. Pucks, fists. They all hurt when they bounced off the old coconut. I waved as he and the Blazer left, and turned my attention back to the professor.

"Okay, now what you're going to do is move into my house for the next two weeks."

I thought of my poor guest room. I had always envisioned human beings staying in it. Well, it wasn't that bad. At least I could burn the sheets, blanket, and pillowcases and that part of the house after he left.

"I will have to go home to get my things."

"I know," I said. "We'll take you there now." As an afterthought I asked, "Where exactly do you live, anyway?"

"In Norwood."

One town over from Dedham. How convenient. Life was getting a bit too ironic for my liking.

"What about my car?" he asked.

"Oh, that's easy. Say bye-bye to it for a while. You're going to drive it home and park it there for about two weeks."

20

As things turned out, everybody was happy with my solution except Kathy. Now that I knew how quick and talented she was, I asked her to ride with Barkagan in his car. Just in case.

Clearly, she was good. Phil would not have sent her otherwise, no matter his sense of humor. She put in her time at the Farm and would do what she had to do when she had to do it. That was the mantra at the Farm: Don't think. Just react and do.

To accomplish that type of thinking and response, one of the first things they destroy at the Farm is your conscience. It took me a long time to get mine back, and it still wasn't right. At times I could still be cold as ice. To friend and enemy alike.

You stay with the Agency for too long, and a little piece of your mind starts to atrophy. It's the part that has compassion. The part that cares. I hoped that it never affected Kathy the way it has so many others. The way it still affects me.

I honestly believe that no other government organization does as much good for the United States as the Central Intelligence Agency. I realize that I am always going to be in the minority when I voice that opinion, but it is something I believe to be fact.

Tragically, while the agency affords you the opportunity to do some good, it bills you for that privilege by causing you to lose large blocks of your sanity and peace of mind. Not so much the employees who work at Langley, but rather, the field operatives. The ones who do the grunt work day in and day out overseas.

With her stint in Afghanistan, Kathy had already set foot in the netherworld where up is down and wrong is right, and had lived to tell the tale. As such, she, like those before her, had to harden herself to a twisted and often fatal reality of life. A reality that dictates that human beings should only be seen as lifeless objects created to further the mission.

While buying into the company line, the smart ones still had to figure out an escape route for themselves for when it was all over. For when they were out. All the way out. It was a trick some could never master. I didn't. I hoped Kathy was better and smarter than me—but time, and pain yet unfelt, would tell.

21

Norwood is a nice upper-middle-class to wealthy suburb of Boston. However, as in many areas, it does have its share of low-lifes moving in. Lowlifes and one rich former defector. The defector lived on Netties Lane, which was just about a half mile down from the town center.

It did not look at all like the kind of street or neighborhood one would find a former Russian defector. I had worked for the government, and I *still* had the impression that they all got to live in villas somewhere in upper Vermont, courtesy of the American taxpayer. Netties Lane, however, with its myriad kids running around, did not bring to mind images of a peaceful green valley in the Green Mountain State.

It was not until later that I found out the professor had a cousin who lived in the neighborhood, and so the defector just wanted to be close to his family. Any kind of family. Defectors have a tendency to get lonely and homesick. Apparently even this one.

After packing the professor up and leaving his brand-new BMW 700 Series in his driveway, we headed toward my home. Along the way, we stopped at a KFC/Taco Bell in Dedham and grabbed three boxes of cholesterol to go. Once back at my place, I checked to make sure the guest room was secure, and told Barkagan to make himself at home.

Barkagan turned to glare at me. "I have no intention of making myself at home, Mr. Wallace. To me, this"—he waved his plump hand back and forth to encompass my home while making a face one has when drinking sour milk—"this home of yours is nothing more than a prison. And you two are nothing more than common guards who I'm sure make not much more than minimum wage."

Kathy tried to jump in but Barkagan was having none of it. "Listen, pro—"

"Listen, nothing!" he barked. "You mistreated me back at my laboratory, and when this assignment of yours is over, I'm going to have you fired. Your government needs me, Miss Donahue. I do incredibly important work for them. Work that your barbaric little mind could not possibly understand. And because of that work, I hold the trump cards. Maybe not right this second, but soon."

He clutched his bag of fried chicken close to his flabby chest and stared wildly at us with his protruding eyeballs.

"So in the meantime, I suggest you both do your small-minded best to protect me and protect the amazingly important work I'm doing for your nation!" With that he took his chicken dinner and his suitcase into the guest room and slammed the door closed. Fine, professor. We can take a hint.

Even though I decided to leave my cat, Gizmo, over at my sister's for the duration of the assignment, I was already missing him. On its worst day, Gizmo's litter box smelled better than Barkagan fresh out of a shower and covered in baby powder.

* * *

Kathy and I ate our dinners in the living room, watching the end of *Roman Holiday*, starring the bewitching and beautiful Audrey Hepburn, on AMC. Afterward, because the sloth was now in my guest bedroom and the other small bedroom had been converted into an office, I made what I thought to be the magnanimous gesture of volunteering to sleep on the sofa. Chivalry, I thought, is alive and well and resides in my heart.

"No," she said. "We can share the bed. It is, after all, your room. You look like the type who can be trusted to keep your hands to yourself."

While far from naïve, I was still somewhat surprised by her response. This new generation was clearly being influenced by the growing lack of morals portrayed on MTV, television in general, and in the movies.

I smiled sincerely as I looked into her dark and amused eyes. "Well, I actually can be trusted. That said, I'm still going to bunk on my sofa."

Kathy trumped my smile with a laugh. "That's kind of silly and old-school. I saw *It Happened One Night*, and Clark and Claudette managed quite nicely. Surely we can inhabit the same bed and still behave."

I nodded my head. "Most likely. But why tempt it? As corny as this may sound, I'm still a big believer in traditional values, respect for women, and the importance of monogamous, meaningful, and loving relationships. Beyond that, I still think that even in this day and age, marriage is the best path taken for a man and woman in love. So, I'm going to crash on my couch and try not to stay awake all night thinking of you all alone in *my* bed. Besides, I'm all out of bedsheets, so I can't put up the Walls of Jericho!"

Kathy slowly shook her head as the smile left her face, to be replaced by a much more reflective expression. "Interesting."

After dinner and an hour or so of mindless channel surfing, it was time for sleep. Or at least rest in my case.

Kathy walked into my room, stood in the doorway, looked back at me for a solid five seconds, and then whispered, "Tsk, tsk, tsk," as she softly closed the door.

In return, I stared longingly at the closed door for half a minute or so, rubbed my face with both hands to snap out of it, then stood to do my security check of the house before parking myself on my small sofa with ESPN *SportsCenter* as my only companion.

22

Six a.m. the next morning confirmed to me not only that Kathy was a morning person, but that her figure was even better than I had imagined.

While contorted into a ball on my living room sofa, I heard my bedroom door squeak. Through the opening popped Kathy wearing a Washington Capitals hockey jersey—a hockey jersey that barely covered the black panties that highlighted her incredible legs and ridiculous tan.

As she glided past me on her way toward the kitchen, I bit my pillow in frustration. With my morals still intact, I closed my eyes and marveled at the quality of God's work of art, which was now preparing our morning coffee.

After a very quick and quiet breakfast, I left Kathy at my house and drove Barkagan to work. I figured as long as he stayed in the building, he'd be safe enough behind the walls of Lincoln Lab. Knowing that, there was really no sense in me hanging around all day. What I saw as I was escorting him through the lobby had me quickly reassessing my almost terminally naïve thoughts.

Sitting in a chair against the wall, thumbing through a copy of the left-leaning *Time,* was a gentleman from the Russian Mafia. He was not wearing a sign saying "Russian Mafia" around his neck. But he might just as well have. I didn't know him, but I *knew* him. I would have known him anywhere. He was former KGB. He was one of Ivanchenko's thugs. Of that I was certain.

He had the stench of death all around him. Its smell permeated the lobby he now occupied. But it was a special kind of odor. It was one that only I could detect. A stench that went unnoticed by the others in the lobby. A stench that nauseated only me. A stench that frightened only me.

Until that very moment, even taking the shotgun blast in Cambridge into account, the whole case had not seemed especially real to me. There was no human face attached to the danger. Sure, I knew Phil was telling the truth and that Barkagan had to be protected. But the element of true danger was missing for me. I was home. I was in Boston. I wasn't in some jungle in Nicaragua or Panama. I wasn't in a prison cell in Lubyanka. I was home. And home was safe. Right?

Clearly, the answer was an emphatic no. Home is no more safe than the jungle, the desert, or a prison. In fact, home might prove to be a more dangerous place to try to survive. Why? Because at home you relax. Relaxing is fine if you've just come back from a sales trip hawking computer software, but in my current business, as well as my old profession, relaxing will see you in an early grave.

Okay, Ian. Time to put it in gear, buddy. That human face of danger was now sitting across from you in the lobby. What were you going to do about this guy? How do you handle a

again. She was like that. In fact, it was why he still held that grudge. He ended up marrying the girlfriend I stole. He stole her back and was pissed off because I didn't try to keep her. Gerry and I grew up as best friends on the mean streets of Dorchester but decades later, that didn't mean he was going to cut me any slack.

"Okay, you can stop rattling your chains," I said. "There's this guy in the lobby of Lincoln Lab in Lexington with two grams of coke in his pocket. He also happens to be with the Russian Mafia. A nice little prize, I should think, for a lowly lieutenant in the state police."

I could hear him drumming his fingers on his desk.

"This wouldn't, by any chance, be connected with a case you're working on, would it?"

"Of course not. I'm merely acting as a concerned citizen."

It took him a few seconds to respond. "Whatever you say, Ian. Should we bust him now, or wait a little while?"

I said, "I'd wait about an hour or two if I were you. I'm not quite sure that he has the coke on him right now."

"I bet," he said. "I wonder what would happen if I searched *you* right now?"

"Listen," I said, quickly changing the subject, "he'll try to follow me in his car when I leave the place. I'll point him out to your guys and then they can toss him when he tries."

Gerry covered the mouthpiece and mumbled something to someone in his office. As he did, I looked up at the sky and watched as a United 757 made a slow turn over "Dot" Avenue. By the time the jet was out of view, Gerry was back to me.

"Gee, thanks for the tip. We'll be sure to do it just your way," he said in a voice that should have ushered in the

Montreal Express as he slammed the phone in my ear. Some guys just never learn to forgive and forget.

I drove back to the beautiful suburbs at something over the speed limit and picked up Kathy at my house. She had since taken a shower and was wearing snug blue spandex Nike warm-up pants and a tight white T-shirt with a sports bra underneath. After hustling her into my car, I explained what I wanted done as we headed back to Lincoln Lab.

"But I was just about to go for a run," she protested.

"Not now. Your country is calling."

"Whatever. Does it make a difference how I plant the coke?"

I shook my head. "I couldn't care less. Just as long as he has it when you're done." She seemed inwardly amused with my answer.

Once there, I pointed out the gentleman to her, and she went into her act. "Oh my God!" she screamed in a voice infused with the flavor of the barrio. "It's Martin Miguel!"

Everybody's head in the lobby swiveled to Kathy. Some because she had yelled. Some because they were in instant awe of this splendid señorita covered in spandex.

"Who? What? Where?" I asked.

"Right there!" she yelled, pointing at the Russian operative and carrying on as if he were the latest Latin heartthrob with five number-one hits. With that, she took off at a dead run for the guy. He looked like he wanted to crawl into the nearest hole and die.

"Martin! Oh, Martin. I love you!" Kathy said as she wrapped her arms around his neck.

"No. You are mistaken, please. I'm sorry. I am not who you think," he said as he tried to pry her from around him. But Kathy was having none of that.

"Oh, *papi*. I know it's you. I'll do anything you want. Really I will. Anything."

As if to prove the point, she jumped up and wrapped her legs around his waist. She didn't even know the guy, and already he'd gotten farther than I did last night.

She was squirming around on his body like a drug-crazed teenybopper. It was all too much for the Russian. He became overwhelmed by the gyrations of Kathy and lost his balance, toppling to the white-and-blue granite floor with her right on top of him.

"Oh, Martin," she moaned, "do me right here on the cold, hard floor. You and me, Martin. Right here!"

He succeeded in pinning her to the floor and leaped to his feet, adjusting his expensive blue suit as he did so.

"Stay away, please. I am not this Martin person!" he gasped.

Kathy got up off the floor and peered closely at his face.

"*Mierda!* You're right. You're not Martin Miguel. That's what I get for not wearing my glasses. Sorry about that, *papi*," she said as she turned and walked away, looking slightly bored.

The Russian was left looking totally confused, with his mouth hanging open catching flies. The guards at the lobby desk located near the elevator banks had eyes only for Kathy and her Nike-wrapped body.

As Kathy walked by, she gave me an oversized wink. I strolled out to the parking lot, where two of Gerry's plain-clothes troopers were sitting in an unmarked blue Chevy. I recognized the driver. Gerry said he was a good cop, so that was that. Gerry could be a prick at times, but he was the best cop I had ever known. If he said this guy was good, then he was good. Simple as that.

I leaned against the driver's side and spoke into the window.

"The perpetrator of the forthcoming crime shall exit yonder building momentarily. When said suspect attempts to follow yours truly, I wish you two fine upstanding young gentlemen to apprehend him. Whereupon, it is my belief, you will find in his possession a quantity of cocaine sufficient enough to prosecute him. Does all of that make sense to you, troopers?"

Carl, the driver, turned to his partner. "See that, George? See what we have to look forward to if we ever become private dicks? We get to talk like assholes just like this guy."

George laughed and took another sip of his Dunkin' Donuts coffee, a brew far superior to the "Star-Yucks" brand of yuppie sludge ubiquitously polluting the world.

George was like me when he drank coffee. He had torn a small piece of the lid, put it back on, and then drank his coffee through the small opening. I don't know why I always did that. I guess because I thought it would stay warmer, or not spill all over me or something. When I was a kid, I heard that truck drivers drank their coffee that way. So maybe that was the reason. Whatever, I was happy to see that George was carrying on the tradition.

"Really, Carl," I said. "This guy has blond hair and is wearing an ill-fitting blue suit. He looks like a football player on an off day. I would guess that he is a very strong individual, and might be armed. I would be careful of him if I were you."

Carl shook his head. "Don't worry, Wallace. The lieutenant told us to put the bag on this joker, so that's just what we're gonna do. As a matter of fact, I think I can see something wrong with his taillights already."

George giggled at that as he pulled a Taser from the glove compartment. I was starting to wonder if he could talk at all. Or only laugh and drink coffee.

"Thanks, guys," I said, turning back toward the building.

I walked back into the lobby and told Kathy to go wait in my car. I then had Barkagan come down and told him we were leaving for the day. He didn't like it one little bit. He wanted to stay at the lab to continue his work.

I quietly pointed out the tough-looking gentleman from Russia, and Barkagan quickly changed his mind. In fact he became paralyzed with fear. He knew better than any of us how his fellow countrymen would treat him if they ever got their hands on him.

I took him out to the parking lot and opened the car door for him. At that moment even a simple task such as that seemed well beyond his capabilities. He was that scared. He kept turning to look over his shoulder. I also kept turning to look over my shoulder. Not because I was nervous, but rather because I wanted to make sure that we didn't lose our shadow.

I got in my Jaguar and turned to look at Kathy, who was in the backseat. "All set?"

She made a face at the back of Barkagan's head and flashed her brown eyes at me. "No sweat. It's in his outside jacket pocket. It was kind of fun putting it there, too. The guy's got a great body."

I scowled at her. "Get serious."

"What's the matter?" she asked. "Jealous?"

I laughed at her. "Don't flatter yourself, sweetie."

She then talked to me in baby talk. "What's the matter, snookums. Did Kathy touch a nerve?"

She may not have touched one with me, but we were both doing a job on Barkagan.

"Please!" he yelled. "Can you two carry on your juvenile antics somewhere else?"

I shrugged my shoulders and looked over at him. "Whatever you say, professor. Just having a little fun."

I drove out of the parking lot and nodded at Carl and George as we went by. They worked hard at ignoring me. If anything, George paid more attention to the honey-dipped doughnut he was eating than he did to me. I don't know, but to me a cop without a doughnut is like a day without a cliché.

I turned out on to Wood Street and was pleased to see the Ivan following me at a safe distance. He was driving a silver Ford Mustang that had, I was sure, taillights that were in perfect working order. But I was also sure that Carl and George would momentarily find something wrong with them.

Sure enough, on came the siren and the blue flashing light on their dashboard. I watched in my rearview mirror as the Mustang pulled off to the side of the road with good old Carl and George right behind it.

Instead of the problem being solved, I saw the incident as a pulsating neon sign warning in unmistakable language that I was just about to get in way over my head on this one. First, Kathy and I playing the part of clay pigeons in Cambridge, and now the Ivan in waiting.

Once again, I had to stop procrastinating. Time to call in the cavalry.

23

How does one go about becoming close friends with a mob enforcer, bodyguard, and occasional hit man? In my case, I simply got a job as a busboy at a high-end restaurant in Dedham by the name of The Roman Forum. As an eighteen-year-old just looking for any kind of money to help support my mom and baby sister while still trying to stash away a few bucks for next year's college tuition, I jumped at the chance when a buddy told me they had an opening at the restaurant. A gig that paid you in cash every day seemed like a great deal to me.

Like a lot of higher-end restaurants of the day, the Forum had a very upscale lounge area bordered on one side by a fifty-foot-long dark mahogany bar mated with matching high-back bar stools, intimate lighting, and truly spectacular looking cocktail waitresses. This was, of course, back in the day when you could say "cocktail," "cockpit," "waitress," and "actress" without some flaming left-wing loon slapping a frivolous lawsuit on your unsuspecting ass.

As a man-child with raging hormones and a deep appreciation for stunning—and highly intelligent—cocktail waitresses, I was very happy when the effeminate day manager assigned me to bus the lounge as some kind of punishment in his belief that I was nothing more than a dumb jock and would therefore receive less tip money in the lounge as opposed to the main restaurant. I was happy to take my chances.

The second thing I noticed after the sensuous curves, full breasts, and long legs was that a large group of very tough-looking men with perpetual five o'clock shadows would gather in the lounge every day at 10:30 a.m.

As the restaurant did not serve breakfast and did not open for lunch until 11:30, this struck me as more than a bit odd. Even more strange, the ten or twenty guys who would assemble in the lounge each morning always trooped in through the back door of the joint, through the kitchen, and then entered the lounge at the far end of the bar where a door was placed for staff to enter and exit the kitchen.

Once in the lounge, a couple of them would instantly slam a few tables together while another high-jumped the bar to start a couple of pots of coffee. Cheeky, to say the least.

The first time I observed this I turned to a fellow busboy whose face looked like a testing lab for Domino's Pizza and asked, "What the hell? What's up with those jokers?"

His cratered, multishade-of-red face instantly went white as he grabbed my arm and whispered, "Shut up, you idiot. They might hear you."

I shook my head in defiance as I scanned the collection of prehistoric hairlines, gold chains, and the inordinate amount of long black trench coats being worn on the cusp of summer.

"Who gives a shit if they can hear me," I asked in a voice louder than needed, my "I'm a tough inner-city kid" voice. "All I see is a bunch of freeloaders sucking down the restaurant's coffee and scarfing down buckets of Goldfish."

"Quiiiieeeet," came the whisper-scream from my fellow

food slave. "They're friends of the owner and they can do whatever they want."

As Pizza-face melted down from a fear I clearly did not grasp, I noticed one of the lounge lizards taking a sudden interest in me.

"Oh, yeah?" I said as I stared back at the guy who was now taking my measure as we stood in the back of the lounge near the jukebox. "Who's the owner?"

Pepperoni with extra cheese started to stutter like a twenty-year-old car on a frigid winter morning in Boston.

"A-a-a-abe V-v-v-valenti."

Whoops.

Even if you existed in the sewer system of Boston and never saw the light of day, you still knew that name.

Abe Valenti. Also known as "Abe the Hook." So nicknamed because that's where most who crossed hum usually ended up. Hanging from a meat hook under one of the various bridges leading into the city.

In more polite and reverential company, Abe Valenti was known simply as the head of the Boston mob. A very bad individual by any definition.

Just as I was digesting that bit of troubling news, the guy who had been giving me the fish-eye stood. And stood. And stood.

Even as a now pretty tough hockey player, I had never seen a human being that big in my life. Ever. He had a neck that would have to be measured in feet and looked like the main support column for the old Boston Garden. His shoulders looked like the run-off parking lots next to Logan Airport.

As the fur-covered building started to make its way toward me, I felt my heart start to race and a giant drop of sweat cascade down the middle of my back. As in, where my spine used to be.

When he was finally directly in front of me, I had to crane my neck up to look at his stone face. As I was about six feet two at the time, that meant that this guy was just a smidge shorter than the Prudential building.

He looked over at the trembling busboy next to me.

"Kevin, ain't you got some napkins that need folding in the kitchen?"

Before the skyscraper even got the word "kitchen" out of his mouth, Kevin was gone and most likely burrowing a foxhole under one of the sinks.

The Missing Link then turned his full attention back to me.

"What the fuck did you just call us?"

When you grow up poor, homeless, and on some pretty mean streets, you tend to lead with your mouth from time to time even when you have absolutely no doubt that it was entirely the wrong thing to do. This was one of those times.

"Freeloaders," I spat out.

A nanosecond later a hand the size of a snowshoe wrapped itself around my neck, lifted me off my feet, and slammed me into the jukebox.

"Tommy," the oldest of the men sitting around the tables said in a measured and somewhat resigned voice, as if this were a regular occurrence, "put him down, please."

Tommy looked back over his right shoulder, saw the older man point to the floor, and then turned back to look at me and smile.

Instead of putting me down as instructed, he more like threw me into the table in front of us like a human lawn dart.

"Tommy," the older man continued in a voice that sounded

not unlike the noise a cement truck makes as it idles in traffic in front of you, "bring the kid over here."

Before I could fully stand, Tommy had placed his left hand in the back of my belt, grabbed the back of my white shirt collar with his right hand, and basically catapulted me the fifteen feet or so between us and the old man. I swear my body did not touch the floor until I crashed into the table and chairs next to the mob coffee klatch.

As I looked up at the older man from under the table from which I was now parked, he pointed to the chair next to him and waved me up.

I crawled on my hands and knees, fully expecting Tommy's talons to snare me at any second and pool-shot me off the mahogany bar, off the front desk, off the ceiling, and into a perfect sitting position in the chair.

When that did not happen, I cautiously took a defensive sitting position in the proffered chair.

While studying a piece of paper with a bunch of numbers on it, the older man said, "What's your name, kid?"

As I was desperately trying to remember my name, Tommy swung his open right hand like a Louisville Slugger and connected with the back of my head. Had he used a closed fist, it would have separated from my shoulders.

As I was staggering back into the chair, Tommy said, "Mr. Valenti just asked you a question, dick-head."

"Ian Wallace," I croaked out.

The mob boss pushed his black-rimmed glasses higher up on his nose and smiled at the guy who had been throwing me around the lounge like a rag doll.

"Tommy seems to think you have been somewhat disrespectful of us."

"Yes, sir," I answered as I flinched, waiting to get smacked again. My flinching made Tommy and some of the other muscle giggle, which in turn made my attitude go from simmer to boil. The change gave me a bit of an edge and helped me to calm down a little.

"You know who I am?" asked Valenti.

"I do now. The other busboy told me."

Until that moment, the guy I had only heard about on the six and eleven o'clock news stared at me for a full ten seconds before speaking.

"And what do you think of that?"

I tentatively lifted my eyes from the floor to his face. When I visually completed the trip I noticed a slight bemused smile on his face. As if he knew exactly where this conversation was going.

"I think you are in a very tough business, Mr. Valenti."

All of the five o'clock shadows and pile-driver necks had now stopped their whispered conversations to listen in. As soon as I realized that, the sweat reappeared on my back and my palms became very moist.

Valenti nodded. "Some days for sure. Like you. Am I right?"

I shrugged my shoulders and remained silent.

"How old are you?"

"Eighteen."

"Who you live with?"

"My mom and little sister."

"Where's your father?"

I shrugged my shoulders again and to my surprise, heard some grunts of understanding from the two tables.

Mr. Valenti continued with his gentle interrogation.

"What do you do with the money you make?"

"Give it to my mom."

"Does it help?"

I shook my head no.

"Why not?

I lowered my gaze to examine the tops of my shoes and remained silent.

Mr. Valenti moved his chair so he could better face me and placed his right hand on my shoulder.

"Ian. We've all been there one way or the other. Answer me. Why doesn't the money help?"

Suddenly, for the first time in longer than I could remember, I was having an adult conversation with a male authority figure. Only this one happened to run the Boston mob.

I felt tears well up in my eyes and I lowered my head even more.

"Because . . . ah . . . because my mom has a drinking problem. Not as bad as my dad, but bad. So she pisses the money away on booze and then we move a lot."

"Evicted?" came the soft, one-word question.

"Yes, sir."

"Eighteen. You in college?"

"Yes, sir," I replied as my nose started to run. Almost as soon as it did, Mr. Valenti gently placed a white cloth napkin in my right hand. I took it and wiped my eyes and then my nose.

"Good," he continued. "Education is a very good thing. I tell these mooks that all the time. If they had stayed in school, they'd all be wearing suits and carrying briefcases today."

The audience of thugs erupted in laughter and stared slapping each other on the back. After a few more gorilla-like snorts of amusement, a voice at the other table said, "That was a good one, boss."

Mr. Valenti shook his head. "Don't pay attention to those guys. They think 'ignorance' is the name of a horse in the fifth race at Suffolk Downs when in reality, it's their state of being regarding most of the world."

"Hey," came another muffled voice. "You don't have to hurt our feelings, boss."

Valenti ignored the comment.

"Ian. Look at me."

I lifted my head and looked into the face of almost anyone's perfect image of a grandfather. Silver hair, glasses, red golf shirt, tan Windbreaker jacket, sharply pressed gray slacks, and black wingtip shoes so highly polished, you could shave in them.

Except for the fifteen or so legbreakers and killers around him, he would be the perfect grandfather in any family sitcom.

Or, in my case, a needed male role model—however unconventional—to offer some wise advice in the absence of my missing-in-action father.

"Ian," said Valenti as he looked around at his crew, "I know you are tough. We know you are tough. It's our business to spot such things and then either deal with it or work with it."

With the words "deal with it" visions of being driven out to the Neponset landfill in the back of a trunk leapt into my mind.

"You are tough," continued the mob boss. "But don't be *stupid* tough. I think you're a smart kid who's been dealt a really bad hand at a very early age. Fine. But never be tough for the sake of being tough. Okay? Analyze every situation and make your move based on that analysis."

Wow. I had only been listening to Mr. Valenti for a few minutes and already he was making more sense than all of my freshman year college professors combined. If Harvard could ever make him dean, they'd finally graduate some educated students.

"Yes, sir," I answered.

Mr. Valenti smiled at me. "This morning you were stupid tough. You did not know who we were. You did not know the situation. You did not know what you were facing. And you did not know how to get yourself out if you got yourself into trouble, which"—he pointed at a couple of still overturned chairs I had bounced off—"you did."

"Yes, sir."

Mr. Valenti clapped his hands together and stood.

"Okay. So here's what's going to happen. I'd like to help create a little college fund for you because education *really* is a good thing," he emphasized for his guys.

"For this college fund," he went on, "in addition to working here in my restaurant, I'd like you to work for me on the side from time to time."

When he saw my eyes instantly widen, he laughed.

"No, no. Nothing bad at all. Just want you to drop off some packages once in a while. Think you can do that?"

"Yes, sir," I answered with the first hint of a smile.

"Great. Stand up, Ian."

I stood warily, keenly aware of Tommy off to my right.

"Tommy," instructed Mr. Valenti, "shake Ian's hand and apologize for your abominable behavior."

Tommy moved toward me and I instinctively took a step back and bumped into the table. More laughter.

Mr. Valenti's number-one enforcer offered me his right hand. I extended mine and as his massive paw enveloped it he said, "Sorry, kid. Just trying to teach a lesson about respect."

We genuinely shook hands as my now bruised-like-a-banana body squeaked out, "Message received."

In reality, Tommy Cappalupo was not much older than me. No surprise, he came out of the heavily Italian North End section of Boston. By the age of sixteen, he had decided that he was going to go into the family business—with a strong emphasis on *family*. Apparently he was a quick study, excelled at his chosen craft, was detail oriented, made the word *unflinching* blush with inadequacy, and prized loyalty to his boss and family above all.

Sandra, one of the cocktail waitresses, told me that a couple of years earlier, she and a few of the other girls stopped in a downtown Boston nightclub to celebrate her birthday. As the women were still in their "work" clothes, which greatly accentuated their many attributes, a group of eight street gang members trying to get lucky at the club started to sexually harass them. When the situation looked like it was about to morph from vulgar comments to violence, Sandra called Tommy.

By the time he arrived at the club, two of the gang members were assaulting one of the waitresses atop the pool table. In less than five minutes, Tommy had killed two of them and put the other six in Boston City Hospital for days to weeks.

All without once pulling out his 9 mm. He inflicted the almost unspeakable carnage with only his bare hands and a pool stick.

Mr. Valenti hired the best defense team in Boston and Tommy ended up serving only six months in the slam for involuntary manslaughter. In truth, if they could have, the

Boston cops would have pinned a medal on his chest for dealing with some of their more troublesome pests.

After my initiation in the lounge, Mr. Valenti would have me ride with Tommy in an incredibly souped-up Jeep Cherokee. Nothing in or about the vehicle was standard, including the sawed-off shotgun resting in a specially built holder on the inside of the driver's door.

As near as I could tell, I was dropping off bundles of betting slips wrapped in plain brown paper. I never asked and no one ever volunteered. At the end of each run, Mr. Valenti would give me a crisp, new one-hundred-dollar bill. It was all the money in the world to me at the time.

Tommy and I also never talked about his job. Ever. We talked Red Sox, Bruins, Celtics, Pats, women, and my amazingly dysfunctional home life. That was it and it was enough to forge a real friendship.

Was I bothered about having Tommy as a friend considering his line of work? On any given day, I was torn one way or the other. I knew what he did and gave a great deal of thought to the implications of his expertise.

On the other hand, no matter how twisted to the outside world, Tommy was a man of tremendous honor. His word was his bond and he would literally step in front of a bullet for a friend.

In the end, God would settle it all out. Until that moment, I was becoming more and more grateful to have Tommy as a friend and a new big brother.

After the close calls in Cambridge and at Lincoln Lab, I slipped off and put in a quick call to big brother.

"What's up, kid?" he asked upon answering the phone.

After all these years, he still had a tendency to call me "kid." I sincerely hoped he didn't do that when we were sharing the same drool cup at the Sunnyside Nursing Home a few decades from now.

I took a deep breath and let it out quickly. "I'm about to walk into a shit storm of epic proportions."

"Personal or professional?"

"Both."

"If it's personal to you, I'm there."

"There be some cash in it for you, courtesy of Uncle Sam."

"Don't matter. You heard me, brother. I'm in."

The former government type now turned tough private detective was about to mist up over the phone and Tommy sensed it.

"Besides," he continued purposely, and kindly heading off the emotion, "we both know you can't wipe your ass without an instruction manual so an epic shit storm naturally calls for a nursemaid, a squeegee, and a hose."

I laughed out loud as I felt several tons of stress fall off my shoulders.

"You got that right. And maybe a couple of those blue plastic ponchos they give you at Niagara Falls."

I gave him the address of Lincoln Lab and asked him to meet me there in an hour.

24

Two days later, with Barkagan safely at work and Tommy now lurking unknown and unnoticed in the shadows, I decided to take Kathy on a couple of field trips that were of some importance to me.

After meeting me to get the data dump on the Russian troll, it was actually Tommy's idea that I go blow off some steam. The big brother trying to look out for me once again.

"You look like shit," he said with his unibrow raised.

"Thanks for the compliment."

"Yeah." He smiled as he continued. "But not like the average shit you back out daily into your toilet bowl, or even one of those festering piles of fertilizer a Great Dane leaves on your lawn. I'm talking that you look as if some prehistoric undiscovered beast crapped you out just before the asteroid hit it in the head."

"So you're saying I look bad," I deadpanned.

"And then some," he laughed. "So why don't you take the tomato out for a date or whatever. I think I can score some Viagra from my old man if anything at this point will help you. You need to decompress and get your mind refocused, my man. You go do that and I'll keep an eye on the walking hemorrhoid."

I have to admit that I felt like that bashful prepubescent boy again as Kathy and I embarked on our "date."

The first part of it involved driving to Northampton to catch part of the Highland games they put on every year. While the main events were not until the weekend, there was still plenty to see today, and I wanted her to get a flavor of a heritage that meant so much to me.

As a boy, my grandparents, with a very strong assist from my mother, had always impressed upon my brother, sister, and me the significance of our Scottish background. For as long as I could remember, we had gone to Highland games around New England and had participated to some extent when we could. Nothing much. Under some degree of duress, we just marched in the occasional opening parade or worked one of the food or souvenir booths.

Like most kids, I did not appreciate what my grandparents and mother were trying to do. In fact, because it seemed they were trying to force it upon me, I rebelled and fought against the indoctrination. Of course, once they gave up, I took it upon myself to learn as much as I could about Scotland, my ancestors, Nova Scotia, and the Highland games.

My dad's dad was a very proud Scotsman from Sydney Mines, Nova Scotia. He was also a very proud Democrat who idolized President John F. Kennedy. As such, he often regaled me with the story of the legendary Scottish regimental band called the Black Watch, and how they preformed for President and Mrs. Kennedy at the White House two days before the young president's assassination.

At the time of the tragic shooting, the Black Watch was on a plane heading across the Atlantic and back to England. Upon learning of the killing, they landed at Heathrow, refueled their jet, and without getting off the aircraft, turned around and flew right back to Washington to participate in the president's funeral march.

To the uninitiated, it should be stressed that this was no high school marching band. Each and every member of the Black Watch was an elite soldier—often a combat veteran—who had been hand-picked from thousands for the honor of representing Scotland in a world-renowned regiment. As an American, and a proud grandson of a man deeply moved by the video of the tribute these men paid to our fallen president, I have never forgotten the gesture, nor the echoes of Scotland that emanated from the bagpipes on Pennsylvania Avenue as they played "Amazing Grace."

To take Kathy to witness the games, and in a very real sense, open a small window to my being, was quite out of character for me. For the last several years, my relationships with women had been few and far between. And when something did happen, I was more interested in running from the emotional.

Now here I was taking a woman I barely knew to an event that meant a great deal more to me than what she would see on the field and inside the tents. Why?

Not being a fan of psychobabble, I did not try to analyze my motives or the situation. Instead, I decided to go with the flow and enjoy the moment and hope Kathy did as well.

Upon leaving the Highland games a couple of hours later,

Kathy turned to me and said, "That was all really quite cool. I especially loved the sound of the drums and the bagpipes. Very moving. The one thing I didn't get was those large men in kilts trying to throw telephone poles around the field. What was that all about?"

I burst out laughing and almost wrecked the car. "Those weren't telephone poles. They are called cabers. And what those large men in kilts were trying to do was to flip them all the way over. A very tough feat considering the caber is about twenty feet long and weighs over one hundred and thirty pounds. Just try picking one up and balancing it, let alone flip it one hundred and eighty degrees. In ancient times, Scottish fighters used to throw them at British fortifications. Today, the caber toss is a symbol of strength, persistence, and skill."

Kathy arched her dark eyebrows. "Have you ever tossed one?"

"Yes," I said with a smile. "Once. And then like the person who solved the Rubik's Cube, I never tried again."

"Fair enough. Okay, where are we off to now?"

"It's a surprise."

As we approached the very large green facility that said "skating rink" on the side, I think Kathy started to figure out what was in store for her. Dazzle her with my hockey skills is what I intended to do. What a teenager I was turning into!

I liked to work out at a skating rink on Route 1 in Saugus. They have what they lovingly refer to as "stick practice" five days a week. From 9 a.m. until 2 p.m., Monday through Friday. Stick practice was just another name for controlled mayhem.

Anybody who had ten dollars, hockey skates, and a stick could take part.

Most of the time, the ice was populated by players I had known for years. I had faith that most of these guys would not try to perform surgery on my person with a KOHO hockey stick. More often than not, it was misplaced faith. The games could get *very* competitive.

Ice hockey, by its very nature, is a sometimes violent, bloody sport. When you have men weighing two hundred pounds, wearing what amounts to razor blades on their feet, carrying a piece of a tree, and colliding in the corners, then sometimes tempers will flare and a fight will ensue.

Because of all the needless fighting that takes place in the National Hockey League, the league is getting an extremely bad reputation. I once had a co-worker at the Agency actually compare the NHL to professional wrestling. And he was serious. He thought that the fights in hockey were staged. Rehearsed by the players before the game.

As someone who once made his living in hockey by fighting, I assured him that every fight in the game was the real thing. It was real blood, real pain, and real stupid.

In retrospect, what I did was wrong. Fighting does not belong in the game of hockey. It only detracts from the beauty of the sport.

After directing Kathy to the hot chocolate machine, I went into the locker room, got into my hockey gear, came out, and hit the ice. As I went through my warm-ups, I noticed Kathy sitting in the stands shivering as the cold mist from the rink wafted over her. As any hockey parent knows, it gets very cold in a hockey rink when you're only a spectator, even in the summer.

Your kid will be warm enough playing on the ice, but you'll swear you're a second cousin to a penguin. I was happy to see that she was at least holding her steaming cup of hot chocolate.

There were six other players on the ice. Odd numbers were always tough on a fair scrimmage. Just then, a large player in a black helmet and blue jersey hit the ice and skated with noticeable power around the rink. As he kept his head down and sent small ice chips flying as he rounded the far corner, the other players on the ice paused momentarily to acknowledge that some talent was about to join the fray.

Five minutes later, with everybody warmed up, we decided to start a game. The way it usually works in these pickup games is that all of the players throw their sticks into center ice, and then one player divides them. One for you. One for me. Most of the time, the teams turn out to be equally balanced as far as talent is concerned. Of course, in these games there are no goaltenders, so you have to improvise. In this case, we piled hockey bags in front of the goal, leaving only about two feet of net to put the puck in.

Having once been a professional hockey player, it was only natural that I wanted to show Kathy how much better I was than the other players on the ice. Fat chance. The fragile male ego was once again in for a thrashing. Only why does it always have to be mine?

The pickup game was no more than ten minutes old when I was all but knocked out by another player behind the net.

In these pickup games there was no hitting. The game could get intense at times, but more often than not, everybody on the ice had a "real-life" job and didn't need to jeopardize it by being stupid and macho.

Knowing that, I had absolutely no worries as I skated

behind our net to retrieve a loose puck. Just as I collected the Slovakian-made black disk on the blade of my stick, I heard first, and then saw, a blue blur coming at me full blast.

I turned just in time to see the very tough-looking player who joined us late coming at my face with his right elbow leading the way.

I tried to get my hands up but it was too late. A minor concussion too late. He caught me full force across my nose and the side of my face. I bounced off the boards behind the net and fell to the ice in a pile.

As I lay there barely conscious, I felt blood pouring out of my nose onto the ice. Just then someone knelt down next to me. Help, I thought, had arrived. Instead, it was one of the Four Horsemen of the Apocalypse wearing a pair of very expensive CCM Super Tacks.

A face leaned down next to mine, and I could smell stale cigarette smoke and coffee scenting some very bad breath.

"Compliments of Vladimir Ivanchenko. Save your life and the life of the whore with you by staying as far away from Dr. Barkagan as possible."

With that, he spit in my face, stood up, and skated away.

An hour after that, Kathy and I were leaving the emergency room of Danvers Hospital. The physician's assistant—*do doctors work anymore?*—told me I had a slight concussion and a swollen but not broken nose. I knew all of that without seeing him, but at least he gave me a prescription for some Tylenol 3 with codeine.

While sitting in the emergency room, I related to Kathy what Ivanchenko's stooge had said to me.

"It didn't take them long to track us down," Kathy said as she gently touched my swollen face.

"They must have got my tag off the Jaguar and then run the number. Bad news for all of us."

Kathy nodded. "No kidding. So what's next, Gretzky?"

I tried to breathe through my nose, but without success. "Beats me. All I know is that guy just made my list. It's one thing to cheap-shot me. But to spit in my face on top of that. That's way over the line. Even for evildoers in the Russian Mafia."

Kathy stood up, leaned down, and gently grabbed both of my hands in hers and slowly pulled me into an upright and locked position.

"Let's go find Dr. Slimeball before Ivanchenko does."

I was going to nod my head "Yes," but I was worried it might fall off.

25

I woke up on my couch the next morning and found I still couldn't breathe through my nose at all. It felt as if cotton lined my mouth and throat. Everything had gone totally dry from breathing through my mouth all night long.

Kathy walked out of my bedroom and headed toward the kitchen. I looked up at her from the sofa with pleading eyes and managed to croak out the word *water*.

Kathy, wearing the tight blue sweat pants and white tank top, stopped her march long enough to gaze down in my general direction and frown. "Pardon me?" she asked.

"Water, please." I sounded like a frog that had a five-pack-a-day cigarette habit.

She shook her head and gave me a look that one generally reserves for maladjusted two-year-olds. "What? The big, tough, show-off hockey player is in pain now? How about showing me how really tough you are by getting it yourself."

"Thanks," I croaked, as I fell off the sofa and crawled toward my bathroom.

* * *

I drove Barkagan to Lincoln Lab and then waited until Tommy arrived. After exchanging the secret handshake and double-checking our decoder rings, I left Sasquatch in charge and headed home.

When I got there, Kathy was dressed and holding the phone out for me. It was Mrs. Casey. She reminded me that I was still owed three thousand dollars from a Mr. Jack Butler, also from Norwood, Massachusetts. Butler was a simple case of a man who suspected his wife was being unfaithful, so he hired me to get the proof he needed to wax her ass in court.

I got him the proof. Showed him the photographs in a restaurant over a cup of coffee and watched him go psycho on me. He screamed that it wasn't true. That his wife loved him and he loved her. That she would never do something like that to him. That I made the whole thing up and that hell would freeze over before he paid me a dime. Then he got up from the table and stormed out of the restaurant.

That was almost two years ago, and I hadn't taken a divorce or cheating case since. Ask any cop, and they'll tell you that the one call they hate going on, more than any other, is a domestic dispute between a husband and wife. Get you killed faster than walking into a bank full of crazed gunmen.

But money is money. And I come from a world where three thousand dollars was, and always will be, a great deal of cash. I had not forgotten that Jack Butler owed me money. Nor would Mrs. Casey ever let me forget. It was just that it was never that pressing, and I never quite found the time.

Butler's story was really quite sad. His wife worked for the postal service at the General Mail Facility in South Boston. A place where more affairs take place than on the pages of any ten romance novels. It was a breeding ground for infidelity.

Very long hours, close contact, and strange shifts all spelled "cheat on your spouse."

Butler's wife was the biggest tramp I have ever known. What would drive a human being to degrade herself with man after man was well beyond my understanding. Possibly insecurity or a need to be loved. Whatever the label, it was a sickness. I honestly felt sorry for the woman.

I had pictures of her having sex in the post office parking lot on A Street. Pictures of her in a motel room on Morrissey Boulevard in Dorchester, getting gang-banged by three low-lifes. Whatever sexual depravity there was, she practiced it. I tried to explain this to Butler. I told him to take their three-year-old son and walk away from her for his and his son's own good. But he was having none of it. He would not accept the truth for what it was. He would rather live with the pain than admit what his wife had become.

Once or twice, I considered taking him to small claims court to get my money. But I dismissed the idea totally. That wasn't my style. I had been in too many courtrooms in my time to drag somebody else's ass through one. The man contracted my services, and I fully expected him to pay me. I still believe in honor. I still believe that your word is your bond, that a handshake is an unwritten contract. Of course, if the honor approach didn't work, then I'd have to lean on him a little bit.

Barkagan was safely under Tommy's watch, and I really wanted to know a bit more about Kathy, so I decided to invite her along for the ride.

After talking about the lovely trees, beautiful streets, and magnificent and expensive houses for a couple of minutes, I decided to propel the conversation into the express lane.

"It's not fair," I blurted out.

"What's not fair?" asked Kathy with a puzzled look on her face. "The very high price of very small houses in and around Boston?"

"No . . . well, yeah . . . that's not fair, either, but that's not what I'm getting at."

Kathy smiled and made a motion with her hands like she was helping to land a small plane at Norwood Memorial Airport.

"Okay. So what *are* you getting at, then?"

I slowed the car to a stop as the traffic signal in front went from yellow to red.

"It's honestly not fair that you know so much more about me than I know about you. You got to sit in Langley and flip through pages of psychobabble bullshit about me and my past missions and all I know about you is what Phil told me."

She turned more in her seat to face me. "Which was *what*?"

"That you were smokin' hot and basically as tough as nails."

Kathy immediately grabbed for the visor in front of her and then pretended to stare at herself in the mirror.

"Well, you're right about that not being much info but at least he *was* spot-on about the smoking-hot part," she said as she laughed at her own joke. "I mean . . . look at me. Yummy."

I laughed along for a couple of seconds as I gently pushed on the gas at the sight of the green light.

"Yeah, okay," I said as I started to study street signs, since I was not entirely sure if I could remember where to turn to get to Butler's street. "I may have noticed your looks and body in passing, but I'm really all about a woman's mind and her intellect."

"Only look at *Playboy* for the articles."

"Absolutely."

"Nice to know I'm with a Nobel laureate who doubles as a celibate monk."

"Monk is a good job. Don't knock it. It was either that or shepherd before I settled on this private investigator gig."

"All right," she said as she let out a long breath. "Anything specific you'd like to know?"

I nodded as I squinted at a street sign that reflected the sun back into my eyes.

"Yup. Tell me about Afghanistan."

The fading smile dropped completely from her darkly tanned face.

"Not much to tell. Was the intel officer for a special ops team and some of our para guys. Was in country for about a year and some change."

"So," I answered with some probing sarcasm, "just routine stuff. Fed the occasional goat, filled out the odd form, snuck in a few rounds of golf in random mine fields. Just a bureaucrat with a badge."

A trace of a smile now reappeared at the corners of her mouth.

"As routine and bureaucratic as it gets when you are tracking Taliban leadership 24/7."

"Do tell," I said as I let out an "I'm impressed" whistle.

"More to come later . . . maybe," she said as she turned her head to look out her window once again.

I shook my head no as I quickly sliced the Jag into a space under the shade of a large maple tree.

I put the car in park and stared across the seat at Kathy.

"Are we there already?" she asked as she looked first at me and then at the house we were now parked in front of.

"No. We are not there yet. And we are not moving until

you give up some more information. Not maybe. Not more to come later. Now, please."

She took off her sunglasses and hit me with that mesmerizing brown-eyed stare. "Okay. So you really need to go there. What I told you is not enough?"

"No, it's not. I think if you were me, it wouldn't be enough for you, either."

Kathy shifted in her seat to face me and then did something I did not expect. She started to cry. Nothing major. But her eyes instantly filled with tears.

Now I felt like a complete shithead. The last thing I wanted to do was reopen old wounds and bring buried pain back to the surface. Phil, and to a lesser extent Kathy, had just done that to me, but my question was not about payback. Anything but.

People not in our business think we are uncaring, unfeeling robots, who know no fear, and have no guilt, no empathy, no conscience. They see some silly movies with some liberal actor playing an Agency or special ops person and buy into that ideological interpretation of the character. It's a gross disservice to the people our nation asks to work in the darkest of shadows amid the most evil of adversaries.

To me and those I know in the business, crying is almost an occupational hazard. More than that, it's God's built-in valve to let off the boiling angst that would destroy us from within if we could not release the poisoned steam from time to time. I had opened Kathy's vent but took no satisfaction from the effort.

"Okay. Fine," she said as she wiped a tear from her cheek. "What do you want to know? That I have always had a weird propensity for languages and picked up Pashto faster than most. That when the Agency learned that I had figured out the language they wanted me on the next plane to Afghanistan because they could not trust the local translators. Do you want to know that after some additional weapons training at Fort Jackson, South Carolina, it was off to Kuwait for even more weapons and convoy training before insertion into Afghanistan? Then you'll want to know that wearing fifty-plus pounds of body armor in one-hundred-and-twenty-degree heat is really tough and that while in Kuwait for training there were no showers, the nastiest of port-a-johns, and nothing to eat but MREs three times a day. You'll want to know that when night fell, we had to sleep on the floor of the same building we had just been briefed in, and that if I wanted to change clothes, I had to do it inside my sleeping bag because there was no privacy. None. Is that what you want to know because—"

I held up my hand. "Kathy. Sorry. Let's just forget I asked and go back to talking about the overpriced homes in the Boston area."

Anger, frustration, and maybe a sense of helplessness seemed to beam out of her eyes.

"Shut up!" she yelled. "You asked. At least have the decency to hear me out."

Indeed I had. I now had to let her get it off her chest.

"You'll want to hear that when I finally got to our forward base, the special ops guys called it Camp Mortarville because the Taliban was dropping mortars on our heads almost every night. And that when I had to stumble from my hooch to use one of the camouflaged port-a-johns in the dead of night because we could not use lights, I had to wonder all the time if one of the locals we employed was going to rape me or turn me over to the Taliban for the bounty. You'll want to know that when I did make it back to my tiny hooch I could never sleep because of either the never-ending gunfire, F-16s screaming by overhead, Black Hawks constantly dropping flares to light up the perimeter to see the bad guys, or all of that at once. You'll want to know that to survive mentally, your new religion became fatalism. If they were going to get you they were going to get you."

Kathy took a deep breath and continued. "You'll want to know that when I went on my very first mission with my team, my very first, we took off in two Black Hawks in the dead of night. That as we dipped and weaved low over the Afghan countryside with no lights, I was terrified and almost pissed myself. That even though I had my M-4 wedged between my legs, an M-9 pistol strapped to my leg, and seven magazines of extra ammo laced into my body armor, I felt completely vulnerable and exposed. You'll want to know that ten minutes into the mission, I saw the trails of light made from RPGs and that one of them hit the other Black Hawk with us. You'll want to know how loud our gunners who were wearing night-vision goggles to observe the dark terrain screamed when they realized they had missed some bad guys. You'll want to know how deafening it got in our Black Hawk when those same gunners then let loose with everything they had in the general area of where the RPGs came from. You'll want to know what it was like when we finally reached the downed Black Hawk and I held the shredded and blood-soaked copilot in my arms as he continually called out for his mom in a softer and softer voice until he was gone. Is that what you want to know?"

I remained silent as I shook my head and felt my own eyes start to water.

Kathy now turned to stare straight ahead but saw nothing.

"Look, I volunteered for the gig. No excuses. But the more we were there, the more we had no idea why we were there. Only that some older white politicians who never served in the military and were never in harm's way decided we should be there. Nation building. Antiterror campaign. Whatever. Someone has to serve and everyone gets to die sooner or later. That was the only unbreakable fact. So there I was. Seven days a week, three hundred and sixty-five days a year. One day blurred into another. No days off. No weekends to decompress. No calling in sick. Wake up, get up, and go find the bad guys. Except for me it was more than that. Because I could speak the language, I was also there to do tribal engagement. What a joke. Those people hated us. We were invaders. We were foreigners. They just wanted to survive. They just wanted to live another day and figure out a way to feed their children. There was no tribal engagement. They were just going to wait us out because they knew—as the Taliban told them—that our civilian leaders who sent us into combat would soon tire of the war or run from it if it became a political liability to them back in the United States. You want to know what I did? I survived a nightmare and got to see hundreds of bullet-riddled or bomb-pulped human beings in the process. So screw you for asking."

As a conversation stopper, that was about as good as it gets.

After a minute or so of looking down at my steering wheel while listening to her breaths slowly settle back into a normal rhythm, I took a chance on speaking.

"I'm honestly very sorry for asking. I am very sorry that I pushed."

When I looked up and over at her, she was still staring out the front window with the glaze of being in another and much worse place covering her eyes.

I reached across the seat and softly touched her shoulder. "I am truly sorry. For . . . everything."

She let out a grunt and smiled a sarcastic smile. "Yeah. Me too. We sure make quite the couple, don't we. Which one of us is the most bonkers and which one has the worst PTSD?"

"Oh, that would be Phil," I answered immediately. "He's *way* more messed up than you and I. Way more."

Kathy let out a deep laugh as she wiped the last of the tears from her eyes. "Yeah, you've got that right. He should be in an institution weaving baskets or cutting out paper dolls."

"Don't kid yourself," I replied with a giggle. "For all we know, he escaped from one."

Kathy lowered the visor to fix her makeup. "No doubt. Okay, back to the here and now and back to business. Or at least your business. Aren't we out here so we can collect the money some deadbeat client owes you?"

"We are."

Kathy finished making herself look even more stunning and then flipped the visor back up with a pop. "Well then, let's go get it so you can afford to buy me a nice dinner somewhere."

26

Suburban Norwood looked very nice in the warm morning sunshine. As luck would have it, when we drove up to his house, Butler was out front doing yard work. God knows where his wife was. Maybe the Seventh Fleet was in town.

He didn't try to run when we got out of the car, so that was a good sign. Kathy's very presence seemed to turn most men into feeble spectators.

Butler was using a weed whacker along the walkway; he promptly put it down when I walked up to him. He looked quickly at my face and extended his hand. "How ya doing, Wallace?"

Kathy stood off to the side, out of personal space range.

I shook his hand and touched my nose. "Oh, not bad. Except for this."

He glanced at Kathy, then looked at my face more closely. "Ah shit, man. What the hell happened to you?"

I noticed one of those giant plastic Red Sox baseball bats at our feet. I pushed it with my shoe as I answered.

"I caught a stray elbow in the nose while playing pickup hockey."

He shook his head and laughed. "Aren't you getting a little too old for that kind of stuff?"

Butler worked evenings for the useless and compromised TSA at Logan Airport and seemed to enjoy doing chores during the day. His lawn looked very green. Too green. Almost like the green you see at Fenway Park or at a golf tournament on TV. The guy also seemed to have a real talent for landscaping. Very neat yard. Too bad the same couldn't be said for his life. Or mine, for that matter.

"Yeah, maybe I am too old," I said as I looked into the eyes of a man in need of peace. "But I'm not here to talk about my childish hobbies."

Butler crossed his arms and tried to look bigger than the five foot seven that he was. "I know why you're here, Wallace."

"Yeah. Because you owe me three thousand dollars."

He sneezed twice into his hand, and discreetly wiped it off on his pants leg. It *was* hay fever season.

"Maybe I do, and maybe I don't."

His attitude was starting to annoy me.

"Look, Butler," I yelled, "I've already proven to you that your wife has been intimate with more men than a building full of proctologists! How much clearer do you need it?"

Before I knew what was happening, he picked up the plastic bat off the lawn and smashed me in the face with it. I staggered back a few feet and grabbed my nose.

Kathy yelped as she ran to my side, ready to lay waste to Butler.

"Aahhhh, shit!" I yelled. "You have *got* to be kidding me. Why the hell did you have to hit me in the nose?"

I reached over and yanked the bat out of his hand. "Give me that friggin' thing."

Butler reached over and touched me on the shoulder. "Hey, man. I'm sorry. It was just a reflex action. Are you all right?"

I tried to stare at him though the tears in my eyes.

"No, I'm not all right, you ass-wipe. You just hit me in the nose with a bat." I looked up at the heavens. "What did I ever do to deserve this kind of grief?"

Kathy looked quickly at my nose, laughed at the situation, and said, "It's bleeding again," before walking back out of personal space territory.

As she did that, Butler was also slowly starting to back away from me. I grabbed him by the front of his shirt and pulled him closer to me.

"No more shit, Butler. Do I get my money or do I have to get medieval?"

He held up his hands. "Calm down. No problem. We can drive down to my bank right now."

I touched my nose and looked down at my hand. Blood.

"You're damn right we can drive down there. Look at my nose. She's right. It is bleeding again."

He looked real fast. "Okay. Just calm down. All right?"

"Calm down?! I got my nose crushed yesterday, and now you smash it in with a plastic bat. *Man*, did that hurt."

I realized I was not acting as the consummate professional and sounded like a whiner, but it *did* hurt.

My sister always said that my nose was too big, so maybe this was really a blessing in disguise. I just never thought that God was into plastic surgery.

During the ride over to the bank, Butler told me that his wife had walked out on him and his son a few months ago.

Transferred to a post office in Florida to be with a younger lover.

"I know I'm better off without her, Wallace. It's just gonna take some time to accept it."

We were approaching Norwood center and its eight million traffic lights. "Yeah, I know. Nobody gets a free ride. Some of us are just lucky enough to experience less pain than others."

He paid me in cash, and I wrote him a receipt. Drove him back to his home and wished him the best. And I meant it. The tough times were still ahead for Jack Butler . . . as well as the rest of us not born into money and picture-perfect family genes.

27

After calling Tommy and telling him I'd relieve him soon, I had a quiet lunch with Kathy. After eating my peanut butter and jelly sandwich and drinking a cold glass of strawberry milk, I was somehow in the mood to exercise. Most people would exercise first and then eat, but why start doing things normally now?

After lifting weights in my basement for fifteen minutes, I was pleasantly surprised to find that my nose was not bleeding. I naturally decided to push my luck and go running. Though dumbfounded by my idiotic decision, Kathy asked if she could join me.

"But of course. Misery loves company and overused clichés."

If I were sorting socks, I would now want her company. The woman was developing a knack for taking my breath away. Which she did again as she walked out of my bedroom after changing into shorts.

Like many truly stunning women, Kathy knew full well that she had a great body and knew how to dress to use that body as a weapon. With that in mind, she liked to wear clothes that would highlight every curve and valley. Nothing wrong with that. A habit more women should adopt. What was wrong with that idea was the confusing signals it sent to me and all basic men. But hey, that's our problem.

She came out of my room wearing a pair of red and white striped spandex shorts. Above those she wore a snug white tank top. Sensuous, chic, tanned, and tight.

"Oh, come on. Why do you have to dress like that?" I asked in real frustration.

She batted her eyelashes several times and answered me in a Scarlett O'Hara–like voice.

"Why, sugar, whatever do you mean?"

We walked down to the baseball field and started running. After about one-quarter of a mile, I had to stop. The pounding had started my nose bleeding again. The elbow and plastic bat had put a TKO on the running for the near term.

I waved Kathy on as I pulled out a napkin from the pocket in my running shorts and dabbed it against my nose. In a matter of seconds, it became bright red with blood. My blood. If this went on much longer, I'd have to have Kathy call the paramedics and air-evac me to Norwood Hospital. I don't think the Black Knight in *Monty Python and the Holy Grail* bled this much when his limbs were lopped off.

As I watched Kathy athletically glide around the field for twenty minutes or so, my mind suddenly played an image on its built-in movie screen of Irena effortlessly skating around a battle-scarred hockey rink years earlier. Just as quickly as the scene had appeared, it vanished. I put my hands up to my face to rub my eyes clear, and was surprised to find them moist with tears. What was going on? For the first time since we met, I was quiet as we walked back to my house.

28

When Phil first offered me forty thousand dollars to babysit Barkagan, I privately thought that was way too much money. My thinking now was that one hundred thousand dollars wouldn't be enough to guard the hairball. Every chance Barkagan had, he busted my chops. This was his way of getting even with us for placing his ugly fat ass under house arrest for two weeks.

I was now on my way back from his house in Norwood after picking up some extra clothes for him to wear. Included in these clothes were four pairs of boxer shorts. Anybody who knows me knows that along with hypochondria, I have a healthy fear of germs. I'm no *Monk*, but I can get ridiculous about it. Such was the case at Barkagan's house. There was no way I was going to pick up his underwear with my bare hands. No way on earth. I was looking around his house for a pair of tongs or something. Failing to find any such utensil, I settled for a couple of paper towels from his kitchen. I then proceeded to pack his underwear as if they were four live rats.

Walking back into my house, I found Kathy sitting on the couch watching the national news on my forty-two-inch flat-screen TV. "Where's Brainiac?" I asked as I put Barkagan's clothes on the end table.

Kathy pointed with her head toward the guest room. "He made a couple of sandwiches and went to hibernate in his room. Hasn't been out since."

I shrugged my shoulders and went in the kitchen to get a glass of orange juice. "That's fine by me," I said over my shoulder. "You're paying me to keep him alive. Not to be his activities counselor."

No sooner did the words come out of my mouth than Barkagan slithered out of the room I would have to sandblast upon his departure.

"Mr. Wallace," he bellowed. The words slid effortlessly out of his mouth, aided by the warm grease that continually lined his throat. "There is no television in my room. If I'm going to be confined to this trailer park dungeon for the next number of days, then I demand a color television and cable so I can watch my shows."

I was in no mood for his shit. "The last time I checked, professor," I snarled, "my cable system doesn't get the Pedophile Channel. I think you want the Catholic rectory down the street."

That got him going. "Ms. Donahue, I demand you make your manservant apologize. Should he not, I will put in a call to the assistant secretary of state and we will see who has the upper hand."

Kathy looked over at me and didn't say a word. Just stared. Thirty seconds later, she was still staring.

"All right!" I yelled to no one in particular. "I'm sorry if I offended him or any of the uncorrupted—but still sex-scandal-denying—clergy left in the Catholic Church doing good deeds that unfortunately don't include protecting the innocence of young boys."

"And?" Kathy asked as she continued to stare.

"And what?!" I asked right back as I shrugged my shoulders.

Kathy pointed toward the professor's room. "And what about his TV and cable?"

I shook my head at her. "You cannot be serious."

Instead of an answer, I got her maniacal stare again. Worse than that, I could sense the professor's protruding eyes also looking at me.

"Fine! Okay! I'll get his television and cable. But guess what? I'm not paying for it. Uncle Sam has to foot the bill for his Animal Porn pay-per-view movies."

Barkagan laughed. "Not only are you a sub-moron, Mr. Wallace, but you are also a cheap bastard."

He went back into his room and, as had now become his habit, slammed the door.

Kathy smiled at me. "That went well. I think he's really starting to like you."

A few minutes later, during a commercial break in the news, Kathy said, "By the way, Romeo. I think one of your airhead girlfriends called twice while you were out."

Airhead girlfriends? Where was the respect? Where was the reverence? "What makes you say that?"

"Because when I answered the phone, whoever was on the other end hung-up. Twice. What do they say? When a woman answers . . ."

As if on cue, the phone rang. I walked into the kitchen and picked it up. "Hello?"

There was no immediate answer. Just shallow breathing.

"Hello, Ian."

Two words. Two short words spoken with a Russian accent made bile crawl up my throat. Made my heart accelerate its beat. I sat down hard at my kitchen table and swallowed several times to prevent myself from throwing up.

"Are you all right, Ian? I trust I haven't caught you by surprise."

Two decades. Two decades since I last heard that voice. No matter the time, it was a voice I would never forget. A voice I would take to my grave. A voice that could still make me physically ill after all this time. A voice I would always associate with only one thing—death.

I took a deep breath and let it out very slowly.

"What do you want, Ivanchenko?" I asked in almost a whisper.

He chuckled. "Oh, I think you know exactly what I want, Ian."

Barkagan. The only reason I agreed to watch the bastard was to get a chance at Ivanchenko. At this point I didn't give a shit about the professor. Or about his research. I couldn't care less about him, national security, or the United States. It was all bullshit. None of it mattered.

The truth was, I never really cared. Phil knew that when he walked out of my office. He knew me. Knew why I agreed. What I wanted. Ballistic missile defense was just a name to me. A concept. Not tangible. Not alive. Not real. In the espionage business, it is well known that nothing becomes obsolete faster than a military secret. Nothing.

And yet men and women die for them. Willingly put their lives on the line. Some to steal the secrets. Others to steal the thunder for God and country. The rest just steal secrets for money and self-gratification. Others are willing to die to protect these secrets. Secrets that will one day prove to be use-less. Obsolete. Secrets that have lost their value long before the bodies of those who have died to protect them have had a chance to cool.

And then there are people like Irena. Human beings re-duced to pawns without their knowledge. Without their con-sent. What she wanted was so very simple, so basic. A state of being most Americans take for granted. Freedom. She only wanted to be free to live out the rest of her life as she saw fit. To get that freedom, she was willing to trade information about Soviet ballistic missile defense. How ironic it was that Phil would bring ballistic missile defense back into my life. A concept that was not yet tangible but nonetheless was ulti-mately responsible for Irena's death, and my hell on earth.

I had lived with the guilt for all these years. Sometimes it was so easy to rationalize why I was not responsible. So simple. It wasn't me who killed her. I loved her. Ivanchenko killed her. Yeah, that was the easy part. Lay it all on Ivanchenko. Maybe that was one of the reasons I wanted him dead. To help al-leviate some of the guilt I had carried for so long now. Guilt I would always carry.

I was Irena's control. Her contact. I was the man who set her up, who allowed the Agency to play God with her life. I had the power to say no, to stop the cycle. I had the power and I chose not to use it. No, I was too clever for the room. I would fool them all. I'd get the information the Agency was so hot for, and I'd marry the woman I loved. Two birds with one stone. But things went wrong. Oh God, how they went wrong.

Time does heal most wounds. Not completely. But a scab will form given time. I no longer thought about Irena as much as I used to. During the last number of years, there had been other women. Most fleeting. Now Kathy had come into my life and the feelings I was developing for her were already very real and very deep.

Life goes on. I know that. I didn't crawl into a cocoon after Irena was killed. I was a realist in a dangerous business. Death is part of the living process. I would never feel quite right about Irena's death. It would always haunt me. Always turn a quiet dream into a nightmare best forgotten. I knew that and accepted it. I really had no choice in the matter. The wound, however, as bad as it was, was healing.

How quickly things change. Phil had partially separated the scab from the skin when he had come to see me. Ivanchenko had just ripped it totally off my body and mind with one swift motion. With just one tool. His voice.

"Ian. I have a deal I would like to propose."

It was so strange. Strange that after all this time, I was still intimidated by his voice. Still frightened by the man. I once again felt as if I were strapped down in a chair in a cold lonely room in Moscow. Once again felt that this man somehow still held my fate in his hands. And maybe he did. My hand shook as I held the phone.

"Ian? Are you still there? Have you lost your ability to speak? If memory serves, the last time we met, you were in fine voice."

I looked down at my left wrist as he spoke. The scar was still very deep. Very vivid. I ran my fingertips over it as I answered him. "Yeah, I'm still here. What do you want?"

"I only want what is rightfully ours."

Kathy had come into the kitchen and stood before me.

She mouthed the words, "Is that Ivanchenko?"

I nodded quickly and waved her angrily out of the room. She shook her head and stood her ground.

"Nothing in this town is yours. Rightfully or otherwise," I said.

"Now is not the time to debate semantics, Ian. I have been authorized by some people I now work with to bid for our property. I suggest you and I meet to discuss it further. It could prove to be quite profitable for both of us."

This was my chance. To put this bloodsucker out of his misery once and for all. Right or wrong did not enter into the equation. The law of the land did not enter into it. The law of God did not enter into it. The only factor that would enter into it would be opportunity. Would I be given the opportunity to put a bullet into the back of his head?

Most people would say that's a very cold way to think about another human being. Monstrous, in fact. But I never considered Ivanchenko to be human. I thought of him as a disease. Nothing more. Nothing less. And disease should be exterminated. Eradicated from the planet for the good of humanity.

I now had him on my home turf and had to use it to my advantage. Bring him someplace secluded. With no witnesses. Sweat had formed once again on my forehead and in my palms. I wiped it off with a napkin lying on the table.

"All right. When do you want to meet?" I asked.

"I think sometime tonight would be best."

I knew just the place. It was a rest stop off Route 128 in Dedham. Very dark at night. And extremely secluded.

"Fine. Do you have someone who knows his way around—"

I did not even get a chance to finish my sentence before Ivanchenko started laughing. As quickly as he started, he stopped. "Don't be a fool, Ian. I have already decided where and when we will meet."

"That's bullshit! Either I pick the place or there's no meeting."

There was no immediate response from Ivanchenko. When he finally did speak, his voice was much stronger. More provoking. "Is that what you *really* want, Ian? If we don't meet, then you'll be depriving yourself of the chance to kill me. Now you don't want to do that, do you?"

Would he always be one step ahead of me? Even in my own country? My own town? Was he that much better than me? Or was his reputation influencing my thinking?

I suddenly felt very tired. Very old. "Where and when?"

I heard his breathing grow louder. "Better. Do you know, ah, I think, Faneuil Hall?"

"Get on with it," I said.

He wanted the meeting very public. Fine. He knew I wanted to kill him. But maybe he was underestimating my determination. I'll take the first chance he gives me. Public or private. I was about done with life anyway.

"Meet me at the Black Rose near Faneuil Hall at eight o'clock."

Click. Dial tone. That's all, folks.

I sat at the table and held the phone in both hands. I simply sat there and stared at the receiver.

Kathy finally walked over, took it from me, and hung it up.

"You're not actually going to meet this guy, are you?"

I looked out my kitchen window at the backyard. A squirrel was making his way slowly toward the house. He was being very careful. Very cautious. He'd stop every few feet and look to make sure a cat wasn't about to end his life. That he wasn't walking into a trap. Maybe he was giving me a message. I liked to feed him once in awhile. He seemed to like Ritz crackers better than anything else.

"No Ritz today, Rocky," I whispered.

"No what?" Kathy asked.

I stood up from the table and held her by the shoulders.

"Yes. I'm going to meet him."

I walked toward my room. Kathy followed after me yapping at the back of my head. "But he could be setting up a trap to kill you."

When I got to my bedroom door, I stopped and looked at her beautiful face and into her dark eyes. "Maybe he is. But I don't think I care anymore."

I quietly closed the door on Kathy and the rest of the world. At least for a little while.

29

An hour later, there was a knock at my front door. I walked out of my room just as Kathy opened it, revealing what must have looked to her like Cro-Magnon man.

I smiled at Tommy as he stood framed in the doorway.

"Well what do you know. It's the missing link, Barney Rubble."

He stuck out his hand. "Hey, asshole. I thought we agreed you weren't going to call me that stupid name no more."

I pointed to Kathy. "Tommy Cappalupo, may I introduce Kathy Donahue."

Tommy leaned in over my right shoulder and whispered, "Does she know I'm doing the job you're supposed to be doing except you can't 'cause you're in lust or whatever?"

Kathy scowled at us. "It's not polite to whisper. Or don't you boys know about proper manners?"

Tommy wiped his right hand off on his black pants leg and shook her hand. "Hey, nice to meet ya. Sorry about the language. And yeah, I got manners."

We sat in the living room.

"So Ian," Tommy said. "How about a brew?"

"Sorry buddy. I don't have any beer."

Tommy clapped his hands together and smiled. "No problem. Knowing what a bore you are, I brought my own."

He had carried a red Nike gym bag into the house with him, which he promptly put on the sofa and opened. Out of this, he produced a six pack of Coors light. His next trick was to pull out a broken down Remington 1100 auto-loading shotgun.

As a proud member of the National Rifle Association and a very strong supporter of the Second Amendment, I nodded my head in admiration of Tommy's hardware and his belief in self-protection. With the current liberal occupant of the Oval Office and his allies in Congress and the media working day and night to take away our guns and ammunition, I sincerely hoped Tommy had more where that came from.

I looked over at Kathy to see her reaction to Tommy's toy. There was none. She acted as if this were an everyday occurrence in her life.

"Kathy, Tommy's a friend of mine. He's going to stay here with you while I go into town."

She arched her eyebrows at me. "Really? Is he the eventual recipient of the extra cash I brought? Is that how he came to be here?"

Tommy went about putting the shotgun together. Totally ignoring us.

"I called him from my room. I thought you could use him."

She moved a stray hair from in front of her now focused eyes. "Why? I'm a big girl."

"That's got nothing to do with it and you know it." I went over and sat next to her on the loveseat. "Ivanchenko has my phone number and clearly my license plate. So I'm sure he knows where I live. He might be trying to get me out of the house so he can drop a hammer on Barkagan."

Kathy nodded at Tommy. "So what's he for?"

"To make sure that doesn't happen."

Tommy looked up from what he was doing, which was sliding shells into the chamber, and gave Kathy his two-hundred-watt smile. "Not to worry, honey," he said as he loaded the shotgun. "It's all under control."

Kathy ran her fingers through her black hair and addressed Tommy. "You can't be serious. If you believe that, then you're almost as moronic as he is," she said, pointing in my direction. She then got up from the loveseat, walked into my room, and slammed the door.

"Don't worry," I said to Tommy. "She grows on you."

He was still looking at the slammed bedroom door with a puzzled look on his face, when he said, "She'd fuckin' better."

30

I parked my car in front of my office on Park Street. At seven-thirty at night, parking in Boston wasn't much of a problem. As long as you could use a spy satellite to find the lone parking spot left in the city, or didn't mind paying a king's ransom to have someone new to our shores scrape your vehicle into a tiny space ten floors below street level.

I decided to take the long way to Faneuil Hall and come in from the back. That meant walking down Milk Street and cutting up Chatham. I had to figure that Ivanchenko would have protection. Where and how many was the question. Who, was not a problem. He would have some of his former KGB flunkies lying in wait for me. I didn't think I'd have that much trouble picking them out. As sophisticated as the Russian Mafia was becoming, they would still have a tough time blending in with the Bostonians and tourists running around Quincy Market.

As I walked slowly toward the Black Rose restaurant in the light of dusk, I thought about death. I thought about my own death. Would I meet my end at the other side of Quincy Market? At some point in time we must all confront our own mortality. We must all die. Most, however, will drift into the cold skeletal fingers of death in the sanctuary of their own home, or under the bland sanitized sheets of a hospital bed.

Others, unfortunately, will suffer a violent death at the hands of a fellow human being. Violence has always been a fascination of mine. What would make one man brutally kill victim after victim, while another would sacrifice his own precious life to save the lives of others? What twist of fate would make Genghis Khan ruthless and Gandhi altruistic?

In cold blood. That is the popular expression. What thought process would end with a human being taking the life of another in cold blood? Good versus evil. Right versus wrong. St. George versus the Dragon. Was it really that simple? So cut and dried. Fiction teaches us that Good will always triumph over Evil. It sounds so nice, so comforting. But it proves to be nothing more than a warm, misguided thought shielding the meek from the chilled misty finality of death.

Reality and experience has taught me another truth. A better truth. And that truth is that evil will almost always triumph over good, unless good is very, very lucky and has a lot of help. The evil men do knows no rules. It knows only the preordained and final outcome. Good, on the other hand, by its very nature, plays by the rules. And that, sadly, is why good will almost always perish at the hands of evil.

As I scanned the faces in Quincy Market, I thought of a poster I had when I was a child. It depicted a giant of a man walking through a peaceful green valley. And on the bottom, it said, in blood-red letters, "I will fear no Evil, for I am the meanest Son of a Bitch in the valley." As I approached my possible demise, I honestly knew no fear. Deep down, I knew the truth. A truth that at times repulsed me. And that truth was that I was Evil. That I would do whatever was necessary to triumph. To survive. That I was not St. George, but in fact the Dragon he sought to vanquish. For at times such as now, my conscience was blacker than the darkest shadow in the most putrid corner of hell. And for that, I was grateful.

A strange excitement burned within me as I went forward to meet and hopefully kill Ivanchenko. It was crowded in Quincy Market at ten minutes before eight. Very crowded. For the most part, it was a young crowd. College age. The adults seemed more at ease taking on the Faneuil Hall area in the daylight. Sunset was approaching and nighttime was for the young. For the men and women with healthy tans and a seemingly unending zest for life.

I wondered what their reaction might be if they knew that a monster was among their number. A monster in every sense of the word. A man spit out from hell as a creation of Satan. A man who would steal their breath away and laugh with the pleasure it would bring him. A man who felt no remorse. Who felt no pity. Whose only concern was completion of the mission. A man who had long since become a machine. A machine that had killed the love of my life, my unborn child, and most of my soul.

I was getting closer to the Black Rose and had yet to spot the Russian muscle. I stopped for a second to study the crowd. A very pretty blonde in white shorts and a maroon and gold Boston College V-neck sweater smiled at me as she passed. I forgot to smile back.

Seconds later, a slightly overweight man in a green Southie T-shirt and gray scully cap walked up and asked me for a light. I told him he was out of luck and tried not to breathe as he walked away leaving the smell of stale beer in his wake.

Nothing. They had to be here, but I couldn't spot them.

He would not come alone. No way. I knew he wouldn't. Ivanchenko didn't work that way. He wanted all angles covered.

Just as I started walking again, something hard jabbed into my right side. I turned to see the face of the guy in the Southie T-shirt and scully cap, inches from mine.

"You move one inch, dickhead, and I'm gonna blow you all over the street."

As I looked at him, someone else took hold of my left arm. This guy was big. Some kind of bodybuilder or something. He had long blond hair and an orange, spray-on tan. Muscles was wearing a yellow tank top and designer jeans.

Locals. Ivanchenko had hired locals to do his dirty work. So much for my theory of him using a few of his former KGB bad boys. I have jumped at so many wrong conclusions in my life that my body is covered with scars. Why should now be any different?

They steered me to a park bench a few feet in front of us. Muscles sat down and jerked me down with him. The guy in the Southie shirt took a fast look around, then sat on the other side of me. Across the street, directly in front of us, was City Hall. A building designed by architects who must have dropped acid just before sitting down at the drawing board. Very strange-looking building. Many Bostonians hated its looks. But not me. I loved it. But I could have picked a better time to admire it.

Southie patted me down for weapons. He quickly found my Sig P250 compact and handed it to Muscles, who hid it in a coat he was carrying. Next we all stood up and they escorted me to an outside table at the Black Rose. The three of us again sat down. Southie kept his gun covered in a jacket and rested it on top of the table, pointing at my chest.

I smiled at him. "So, you kids come here often, or is this your first date?"

Muscles grabbed my left wrist. "If I was you, I'd shut the fuck up."

A slightly overweight waitress in black jeans and a white shirt came over to take our order. Southie told her we were waiting for someone and to come back later.

I was trying to appear calm, but inside I was doing a slow burn. I had come here with the express purpose of killing Ivanchenko, and instead had had my gun taken away from me like I was some kind of a green rookie. Which is just what I had acted like. I had assumed Ivanchenko would use Russian personnel. Assumptions like that get people killed.

A shadow fell across the table. As it did, Muscles stuck his gun in my side, just to remind me that he was still there. I took a very deep breath, let it out slowly, and looked up at the shadow caster.

Dapper. Very dapper. Dressed to the nines. Would have made a fine cover boy for *GQ*. Expect for that nasty scar running down the side of his face. He was wearing a charcoal gray suit—Armani, I was guessing—white shirt, yellow tie, gold collar bar, and diamond stick pin.

There was an air about the man. Something that pulled your eyes toward him. It seemed almost all the men and women at the tables around us were trying to look at him without appearing to do so. Especially the women. Maybe they were attracted to his strength. When I was with the Agency, they had Ivanchenko rated as possibly the most dangerous man in the world. Overall, he had killed more people than bin Laden. No amount of expensive clothing or smooth talk would change that.

When I finally looked into his eyes, it was like looking directly into the eyes of defeat. My defeat. And he knew it.

"How are you doing this fine evening, Ian?"

I did not answer him. I had nothing to say. I was empty. I had come here to kill him, and I had failed. He pulled out the chair and sat opposite me.

"Ian, I will not be coy about this. You have an item we want very much. I have been authorized to bid for it. What would you say would be a fair price?"

His jacket size had to be at least fifty-two long, and still it seemed tight on him. I looked into those dead eyes and shook my head.

"I will not play games, Ian. You and I both know the Cold War never ended. And with what's going on in Afghanistan, the Middle East, and here in the States, it may soon be back with a vengeance. So why not set yourself up with some money for the coming chill? I can pay you five hundred thousand dollars for our property."

Muscles and Southie smiled a knowing smile at each other. They would happily put my body in a tree shredder for a fraction of that amount.

I once again shook my head. This did not please Ivanchenko. He slammed his fist down on the table. To my amazement, it did not split in two. He did, however, succeed in causing quite a few nearby patrons to almost jump out of their skin.

"You are a fool, Ian!" he whispered. "My offer to you is genuine. You have learned nothing in all these years! What you did to my man the other day was amateurish. Remember this night when it is your time to die. I will now do what I must. What you have *forced* me to do."

He got up and started walking away.

"Vladimir," I finally said.

He turned slowly to face me. There was a smirk on his face. "Yes, Ian?"

I stood up from the table. Muscles and Southie stayed where they were. Their job was just about done.

"I'll see you in hell."

The smirk vanished from his face. A chill ran down my spine as he stared at me. It was all I could do not to close my eyes.

"Yes." He smiled. "I believe you are right. But I fear it will be you welcoming me. Your time is close."

He then spun and walked off through the crowd. Fifteen minutes later, I was let off my leash by the locals and went home.

The next morning, the *Boston Herald* had a front-page story about two bodies being pulled from the canal next to the Gillette building in South Boston. There was no immediate identification, but one of the men was wearing a green Southie shirt. Good-bye, boys. Paid in full by the Russian Mafia.

31

Everything was strangely quiet and routine for the next few days. The calm before the bullet. The whole situation made me so nervous that I decided to attend to the ton of paperwork Mrs. Casey had piled up in my in-box at work. So as not to be alone in my pain, I brought Kathy in with me while Barkagan was at work and Tommy was swinging from tree to tree nearby looking for bananas to eat to break up his boredom.

First things first, however. Before going up to my office, I finally got around to depositing my money from the Agency.

I went over to a Bank of America on Franklin Street and broke up what would have been a very boring day for the tellers by having them speculate on how a peasant like me could come up with forty thousand dollars in cash.

Kathy and I then walked to my office. Standing in front of my building, basking in the warm sunshine, was one of my favorite people. She was a "bag lady" and her name was Barbara. I'd asked her more than once what her last name was, but she'd never tell me. She was about sixty-five years old and lived out of the shopping cart that always accompanied her. It contained all of her worldly possessions, which were few indeed.

You could see that at one time she had been a very attractive woman. But her years on the streets had taken their toll. Even with all of that going against her, she still carried herself with grace and dignity. She was a proud woman. A woman with bright, clear blue eyes. Eyes that were warm. Eyes that held compassion for everyone, including those who crossed the street to avoid one of the "unwashed masses."

She had told me once of a husband who used to beat her senseless, and finally left her alone with two small girls to raise. A man who was a useless alcoholic and who attempted to recapture some of his lost self-esteem by beating on a defenseless woman.

After a few years, the strain of supporting and raising two young girls by herself became too much for Barbara. She realized that she wasn't cut out for the task, and that the children would be much better off staying with extended family. I often wonder if her living in the streets was a form of self-punishment for giving up her children. I felt so very sorry for the woman. And yet, she still had her pride, so I tried to treat her accordingly.

"Hi, Barbara," I said. "I'd like you to meet a friend of mine. This is Kathy Donahue."

Barbara turned to smile at Kathy.

"Let me tell you something, young lady. If you have Ian here as your friend, then you have the best friend a person could ever have. You should consider yourself a very lucky woman. He tries to pretend that he's a tough guy, but in reality, he is the most compassionate person I have ever known. He goes out of his way to help out the less fortunate in this town. And then he keeps it to himself. He is a very special person."

Kathy shook Barbara's hand, and turned and looked at me as if seeing me for the first time.

I said, "Stop it, Barbara. Let's not exaggerate to the nice lady." I then bent down, kissed her gently on her dirt-smudged cheek, and whispered, "I love you, sweetie. Let me know if you need anything."

Life was so unfair.

As we entered the lobby, Frank's eyes almost popped out of his head when he saw Kathy. She was wearing a pair of very snug white pants and a black vest with no shirt, just a black bra underneath. She had caused quite a few cases of whiplash in the male population of Boston on the streets between my office and the bank.

For an old guy, Frank seemed to have an awful lot of hormones still running around in his body. He stood up and eyed Kathy hungrily as we approached. I made the introductions once again. "Frank, this is Kathy. Kathy, this is Frank."

I watched as they shook hands. I had seen Frank meet some of my female friends before, so I knew what was coming. Frank did not like to let go.

I could see Kathy trying to pull away as he pumped her hand for the tenth time. "It's very nice meeting you, Frank," she said. Nice try, but no soap, babe. He just kept smiling at her and shaking away. I finally rescued her by pulling his hand away from hers. I'm not saying it was easy, either. For an old guy, Frank could exhibit superpowers when needed.

As we walked into my office, Mrs. Casey was just closing a file drawer. "Well, well, well," she said, looking quite prim and proper in her gray high-collared dress, with just a hint of blue showing in her still dark hair. "Look who finally remembered where he works."

She gave Kathy the once-over as she stood next to me. "Who's this?" she asked in her still strong English accent. "Some tart you picked up in a pub last night?"

Kathy laughed. "I like her."

Kathy crossed to the other side of the office and introduced herself to Mrs. Casey. The two of them began talking in hushed tones while glancing at me every few seconds. Their gossip was broken up only by their laughter as they continued to look in my direction.

"Fine," I pouted. "I don't have to take this treatment. There are plenty of people better than you two who want to abuse me. So get in line. I'll be in my office if you need me."

That statement only made them giggle all the more. Women. When will they give me a break?

32

I went through my mail for the next half hour. Most of it was bills that read "FINAL NOTICE!!!" or brochures from electronics companies telling me that their latest gadget would enable me to hear a flea pass gas at four hundred yards. A thrill I could wait a little longer to experience.

There was also an email from Tiffany down Virginia way. As I read it, I was amazed to find that the computer had not melted from the contents inside. The girl had a very active and sensuous imagination. Even more outlandish was the nude photo she'd attached. Interesting tattoo on her right hip. Too young and wild for me, though. I deleted her porno-gram immediately in case the host of *To Catch a Predator* was monitoring my emails.

After another ten minutes of making busy, I heard my intercom buzz.

"Yes, Mrs. Casey?" I said.

"Frank is on the phone, and he says that there is a gentleman downstairs waiting to see you."

That was interesting. I wasn't expecting anyone today.

"Did Frank say what this gentleman wanted?"

"No. Only that it was personal and very urgent."

A sixth sense told me that this was going to be trouble.

"Okay. Tell Frank to send him on up. And ask Kathy to step into my office, please."

As I hung up, Kathy walked in and closed the door behind her. I looked at her. "Something doesn't feel right about this. I want you to sit in the far corner over there and keep your hand on your piece. But keep it inside your purse. No sense in scaring the snot out of this guy if he's a possible paying client."

She took one of the two chairs from in front of my desk and sat in the corner with her purse on her lap.

A few minutes later there was a knock on my door and Mrs. Casey showed the "gentleman" in. He was definitely not here to sell me night-vision binoculars, although I was more than willing to bet that he had used some from time to time.

"Thank you, Mrs. Casey. That will be all," I said.

She flashed me a nervous glance as she quietly closed the door behind her. I studied the man before me. He was young, about twenty-eight. Very athletic-looking. About five foot eleven and 185 pounds. He was wearing a blue blazer with gray slacks. Travel to the United States since the breakup of the Soviet Union had certainly improved the dressing habits of these heretofore crude Russians. He had yet to say anything, but he was a clone of the one from Lincoln Lab a few days earlier.

"Do you speak English?" I asked, knowing that he did.

He smiled at me and then turned to beam his pearlies at Kathy. Just to let us know that he was aware of her presence.

"Oh I speak English very well, Mr. Wallace. Much better, I am told, than you speak Russian." He kept right on smiling. Just like a person who knows that he is in the driver's seat. It was a very arrogant little smile.

I said, "Oh, I don't doubt that you do, Mr., ah . . . ?"

"'Putin' will work for now."

Nice. He had a bit of a sense of humor.

"Of course. Now, how can I help you, Mr. Putin?"

He walked closer to my desk. I could see Kathy slip her hand into her purse behind him.

"I need no help, Mr. Wallace. I have only come to deliver a message."

Why did I think that I was not going to like what he had to say?

"Colonel Ivanchenko wanted me to extend his warmest greetings to you. And to tell you that your job is now complete. We will now ensure that Professor Barkagan comes to no harm." He laughed as he went on. "Well, at least no further harm . . . for the moment."

He slipped an aluminum cigar tube out of his inside coat pocket and placed it on the desk before me.

I stared at him for about five seconds, and then opened the tube. It was all so pointless. It was Moscow all over again. Only this time, the sadist Ivanchenko was in Boston.

As I took the top off and looked inside, my mind flashed to Tommy. If this creep was telling the truth, that meant Tommy was either dead or in very bad shape. No way these guys could ever get by him. Not on their best day.

So, if they had put the bag on Barkagan, then they would have had to kill Tommy to do so. The very fact that Tommy had not called in the alarm basically confirmed that outcome.

As numbness, rage, and resignation started to settle in upon me, I looked inside the tube. It was packed with rolled-up gauze. I pulled the gauze out and looked at it. The bottom was caked in dried blood. I looked up at "Mr. Putin." His unnaturally blue eyes were dancing inside his head with an animated excitement. Another psychopath.

I pulled open the gauze. The bottom was stuck together, so I had to rip it. When I had it open, I was staring down at a human finger. It looked to be a pinkie finger. It really came as no surprise. That was the Russian Mafia's style. They were ruthless and learned it all from their days in the KGB. I had once heard that when four of their diplomats in Beirut had been kidnapped by a fanatical group of Muslims during the Cold War, the KGB got them all back unharmed within forty-eight hours. They simply kidnapped the brother of the leader of the terrorist group and then sent the leader a different body part of his brother every hour on the hour. Very effective. We could still learn a lot from these guys, in my opinion, as we confront our own increasing threat from homegrown terrorist organizations.

"Is this supposed to mean something to me?" I asked.

He continued to smile down at the finger. He wouldn't be here if they didn't have Barkagan. If they hadn't killed Tommy. That was the professor's finger lying there decomposing before my very eyes.

I picked up the phone and dialed the number for Lincoln Lab. While I was doing that, Mr. Putin started quietly humming something horrid by Miley Cyrus. They give us beautiful ballet, we give them vapid ignorance with off-key voices. So much for cultural exchanges.

The receptionist told me that Barkagan had left the building with two gentlemen from the State Department a few hours ago. With the emphasis being on "State." Sure thing. I next dialed Tommy's cell phone. It went straight into voice mail. I gently put the phone back in its cradle.

"Okay," I said, letting out a very long breath and looking up at the Russian. "What's the deal? What do you want from me?"

For the first time since he entered my office, the smile left his face. "We want nothing from you, Mr. Wallace. We only want you to know that what was once yours is now ours. We only want you to know that you can't treat our people as you did the other day and expect to go unpunished. We only want you to know that your time is coming, just as it did for that bitch a few years ago in Moscow. You remember that, don't you, Mr. Wallace?"

He turned and walked toward the door.

"Wrong thing to say, comrade." I said.

It's never too early to start teaching a reprobate proper manners. He stopped and turned to face me. His ever present smile was still firmly in place. But not for long. He stared down at my right hand and the smile vanished from his face. My hand was resting on my desk, and it was wrapped around the Sig P250 I had just pulled out from my right-hand desk drawer.

"Some people," I snarled, "just never know when to button their lips. And guess what, Boris? You're one of them."

He was definitely not smiling now.

"You cannot do anything to me. I have diplomatic immunity."

I got up and walked around to the front of the desk.

"Hey, no kidding. Is that right? Well, let me tell you: I'm impressed." I turned to look at Kathy. "Aren't you impressed, Kathy?"

She smiled but never took her eyes off the Russian, nor her hand off the pistol concealed in her purse.

"Kathy, come here and search this bag of vomit."

I could see him tense up as Kathy approached.

"Go ahead, Mr. Putin. Make any kind of move," I begged, thinking of all Tommy had done for me over the years.

He was too smart to try anything. But he wasn't above throwing some rhetoric my way. "Things are not done this way in the United States. You have laws you must uphold. You are a representative of your government. Your president is a social-ist. This is illegal."

Kathy's search produced nothing. He was just Ivanchenko's messenger boy. A peon. But he could prove to be a very useful peon.

I said, "Well, you're right and you're wrong. You're right in that what I'm doing is illegal. But you're wrong when you say that I'm a representative of my government."

He looked confused. And was beginning to look scared.

"I used to work for the government," I explained. "I am now in private practice. And what that means is that your little gangster ass is now in a sling."

Beads of perspiration were now starting to form on his forehead. "I warn you again," he said nervously. "I have diplo-matic immunity. You must do nothing to me. If you do, it will be a crime against the Russian Republic."

The guy sounded like a broken record. "Yeah, yeah. I've got it. You may have diplomatic immunity, but all that proves is that your government is in the bag of the Russian Mafia. As far as I'm concerned, you're still nothing more than a low-level criminal puke. Now just shut the hell up and sit down in that chair."

I pointed to the lone remaining chair in front of my desk. He was showing a marked reluctance to obey my direction, so I drove my right fist into his stomach to help improve his disposition. The breath exploded from him and he doubled over in pain.

"That's right," I said as I sat him in the chair. "That's a good little killer." I hoped he had a strong tummy and didn't throw up all over my rug, or Mrs. Casey would come in and be forced to do just terrible things to him.

With Mrs. Casey in mind, I turned to Kathy. "Kathy, go out and tell Mrs. Casey that I won't be needing her anymore today. And that she can go home. Don't let her come in here. And wait out there to make sure that she leaves."

I stopped to look at Mr. Putin. He was starting to get his breath back. Good recuperative powers. Probably would do well in the swimming events in the Olympics. I wondered how long he could hold his breath if I wrapped him in chains and dropped him to the bottom of Boston Harbor? He might set a world record, but who would know?

I continued instructing Kathy. "After Mrs. Casey leaves, I want you to go down to the *CVS* store on Tremont Street and pick me up a roll of duct tape and a new Bic cigarette lighter. I know you've got one but we need a full one. If they don't have duct tape, then make sure you pick up something strong."

I looked down at the Russian, who was now looking up at me. "Very strong," I said to her as she went out the door.

I stuck my gun in his right ear and tore some skin. "Tell you what I want you to do, champ. I want you to place your hands to the back of your head and lace your fingers together. Do you think you can do that for me?" For a little added emphasis, I ground the barrel into his ear. He let out a yelp and put his hands behind his head.

"Thank you," I said. "You know, in a little while, you're going to experience more pain than you have ever known in your lifetime. More pain than you can imagine. You can save both of us the time and trouble if you just tell me where Professor Barkagan is being held."

He shook his head. He may have only been a messenger boy, but I had the feeling that he was a tough messenger boy. But then, he could afford to be tough. He didn't know what I had planned for him.

"Your boss made a mistake sending you here. You see, he likes to rub things in. And that's a flaw in his character. Hopefully, a fatal flaw. Because now I've got you. And I'm going to wring you dry. So how about it? Where's the professor?"

Nothing. I was now on the receiving end of the silent treatment. He started to move his hands from the back of his head, so I smacked him across the side of the face to remind him not to do that.

When I was with the Agency, a few of the people who worked in my department could run a little on the sadistic side. I was no exception. Just throw a switch inside your head and a fellow human being becomes nothing more than a piece of meat. What I was about to do this time was not the "waterboarding" that got the liberal terrorist sympathizers all fired up, but was outright torture in every sense of the word. But I wanted Ivanchenko. And to get him, I'd walk through the gates of hell and kick the devil in the balls if I thought it would help.

Several minutes later, Kathy walked back into the office. "Got 'em," she said, holding up a thick roll of silver duct tape and a yellow Bic lighter.

A few seconds later she let out a scream as Tommy half stumbled into the office holding a handful of blood-soaked napkins to his neck.

33

Holy shit," I said in relief as the sight of him made my knees start to wobble. Way too much adrenaline was now flowing through my body.

As I moved to steady Tommy, Mr. Putin tried to make a run for it. Kathy hit him three times in the face and throat and he hit the floor like a number-ten bowling pin.

I then guided Tommy over to my sofa, where he promptly collapsed.

"Man, am I glad to see you," I said, smiling as I patted his right arm, which had as much give as a block of marble.

"Tell me about it," he said with a painful chuckle.

"What happened?" I asked as I looked over at Putin, on whose back Kathy's right foot was resting firmly.

Tommy slowly shook his head. "Not really sure. One second I'm sitting outside the lab sipping my coffee in the front seat of my car, the next a Lexington cop car pulls up beside me. I see a bright flash out of the corner of my eye and that's about all I remember."

I shook my head back at him. "Not a real cop car."

Tommy smiled then winced in pain. "Yeah, that's the vibe I'm getting now."

"Silenced pistol."

"Yup. What I would have used."

"So, they have the professor."

"Yeah. Sorry about that."

"Sorry," I countered. "Please. I'm the one who owes you an apology for dragging you into this nightmare."

Tommy held up his right hand. "Shut it. I volunteered. Remember?"

He then slowly brought down the napkins from his neck and studied their deep crimson color. "Of course, I now *will* be taking that government money you offered."

"And then some." I laughed.

"And then some for sure."

"Well, thank God whoever Ivanchenko sent to hit you was a lousy shot and that your neck is made out of titanium."

"Yeah. Okay. Whatever. Just no Flintstone jokes right now. I ain't in the mood."

I walked over to my desk, opened the bottom left-hand drawer, and pulled out a fairly sophisticated medical kit.

"Let's get your wound cleaned, sanitized, and properly bandaged. We can get you to a hospital later."

Tommy held up both hands. "Ian, are you a complete idiot? What are you thinking? No hospitals. No reports. No nothin'. My uncle Sal is an internist and lives over in Eastie. After we deal with this piece of shit, I'll have him take a look at my neck."

I pointed at Putin and looked at Tommy. "Speaking of that, you up to it?"

He stared at Putin with a look that made the hairs on the back of my neck stand on end.

"Try and stop me," he said in a tone I had never heard.

It took about five minutes to attend to Tommy's wound. The bleeding had mostly stopped but it looked like the bullet had taken about a half inch of flesh with it. Better to have his uncle check him out later.

When I was finished with my amateur patch job, Tommy was clearly getting his energy and bearings back. He truly had the constitution of a Brahma bull.

"What you got in mind for the mook?"

"I think you know."

"Yeah, that's what I figured," said Tommy, nodding. "The professor is not going to last long so we're going to have the make the mook squeal real fast."

I walked over and put my hand on Kathy's shoulder. "We've got it from here. Why don't you go for a fifteen-minute walk around the block a couple of times."

Kathy looked down at Putin, whose eyes were getting as big as saucers.

"Why? What are you going to do to him?"

"Absolutely no imagination needed here. Just make him talk in the quickest way I know how."

Kathy shook her head. "So, you're going to lower yourself to their level by torturing this guy."

I felt my face flush with the anger I was now feeling.

"You have got to be kidding me," I said to her. "You're going to go all morals on me? Now? Here? Take a good look at that finger on my desk. Take a good look at Tommy."

"Ian—" she started to say before I cut her off.

"Wait," I went on in a raised voice. "You people brought me into this. You people ripped off my scabs. I was minding my own business until Phil . . . and you . . . walked through my doors with this assignment."

Kathy moved closer to me, until her face was just inches from mine.

"You're right. Now is not the time. Later. Later . . ."

She turned and started to walk toward the door. "And I'm not some little girl you can order around. I'm not taking a walk anywhere. I'll be sitting at Mrs. Casey's desk if you need me."

"Suit yourself. Just close the door behind you."

After she left with the now predictable door slam, I clicked my mind back to the here and now.

"Let's go, maggot."

I grabbed Putin off the floor and threw him back into the chair. He and the chair toppled over from the force. That was the idea. Had to reestablish dominance and fear.

I motioned Tommy over to me as I picked up the Russian again and planted him back in the chair.

"Listen," I said to Tommy. "This is going to get very ugly in a minute. But I need your help. This guy's going to be bouncing around pretty good in his chair and I need someone to make sure that he doesn't fall over. Are you up to it?"

His lips were pressed tightly together as he gazed at the Ivan, who was straining to comprehend our conversation, without appearing to do so.

"Payback is a bitch," said Tommy as he patted the Ivan on the top of his head.

I grabbed the thug by his hair. "Last chance, Mr. 'Putin.' You going to tell me where the professor is or not?"

Zip. Okay. I tried. My conscience was clear. I would now play the game by Ivanchenko's rules. What I was about to do was a little trick they taught some of us down on the Farm. I'm told that the KGB used the exact same method in Afghanistan before we got there.

The technique I was about to employ is a guaranteed way of extracting information in the shortest amount of time. As long as you didn't care what condition you left your victim in.

"Okay, pal. I want you to take off your shoes, pants, and underwear. And I want you to do it right this second." I struck him hard across the face again with the back of my hand. When you begin to interrogate a subject, it is very important that you create a sense of hopelessness in that person. That his very life is in your hands and to make him understand beyond a shadow of a doubt that it means less than spit to you.

"Tommy, go out to Mrs. Casey's desk and bring in those phone books she has in the bookcase next to it."

By the time Tommy came back in, the Russian was sitting in the chair, minus his shoes, pants, and underwear. At least he wasn't the modest type. He didn't try to cover himself. Of course, the fact that he was too scared to move his hands from behind his head may have contributed to his lack of modesty.

"All right, Boris. Here's what we're going to do. I want you to slide forward in the chair until I tell you to stop."

He found his voice. "Why must I do such a thing?"

I grabbed him by his hair and screamed, "Because if you don't, I'm gonna shoot you! Let's go. Move your ass."

He started to slide forward.

"Stop," I said. I backed away and looked at Tommy. "You got your nine?"

He nodded in the affirmative.

"Good. Put it in his mouth. If he moves, pull the trigger."

Tommy put his gun up to the Russian's face, but he would

not open his mouth. I was just about to help him out when he jabbed two fingers into Putin's solar plexus. As the Ivan opened his mouth to get air, Tommy stuck the gun barrel in.

"Cute," I said.

I picked up the three phone books and jammed them between the Russian's back and the back of the chair. I didn't want him to be able to slide backward once I started. I reached for the duct tape and taped each of his arms to the arms of the chair. I then taped his ankles to the bottom of the chair legs. I was very generous with the tape. I didn't want him breaking free.

I had him positioned so that his penis and scrotum were now hanging free from the chair. I think it was beginning to dawn on him what I now had in mind.

"Please," he pleaded. "Do not do this thing. I cannot tell you anything. The colonel would have me killed."

I shook my head. "Well, that's where you're making a big mistake, Boris. The colonel's not here right now. I am. And while the colonel might kill you if he finds you, I *have* you, and I *will* kill you if you don't tell me what I want to know. So, once again, where is the professor?"

He shook his head back and forth. I took a handful of tissue paper and stuffed it in his mouth, and then taped it closed with a few feet of the duct tape.

"Tommy, stand behind him and hold him down by the shoulders. Hold him as tight as you can."

Tommy moved behind him and placed his hands very firmly on the Russian's shoulders.

I got down on one knee before him and showed him the Bic lighter as I turned up the flame as high as it would go. The sweat was pouring from his forehead. Never in his wildest dreams did he expect Americans to act like this. Well, welcome to the world after September 11, Mr. Putin.

I put the flame under his testicles and his reaction was immediate. Tommy had all he could do to hold him down. The smell of burning flesh and pubic hair was nauseating. I thought I was going to lose my lunch.

Ten seconds later I knew where to find the professor. The very reality of the process starting was enough for him to immediately snap his head up to look at me with broken eyes and a broken spirit. Even though he did get singed, he suffered virtually no real harm other than the mental anguish that was sure to haunt his mind for quite some time to come.

They were keeping Barkagan at the Harbor View apartments until they could suck as much of his money out of him as possible, after which they'd execute him and dump his body somewhere. A task Ivanchenko would relish.

My immediate problem was how to get rid of the wounded duck. He was in no condition to travel on his own. In fact, more from acute stress than the brief pain he felt, he was barely conscious.

I decided to try my luck once again with Gerry. I picked up my phone and punched in the ten numbers from memory. "Lieutenant Donovan, please. Tell him it's Ian Wallace."

This time Gerry was on the line in seconds. "Do you know what the fuck you did to me, asshole?!"

Maybe calling Gerry was a mistake.

"Gerry. Calm down will you? What are you talking about?"

He was not about to calm down. "You want to know what I'm talking about? I'll tell you. I'm talking about the State Department crawling up my ass because of the Russian you had us put the bag on. I'm talking about taking shit from my captain because of the heat I brought down on our barracks. I'm talking this guy had diplomatic immunity, and the Russians raised all kinds of hell down in Washington, and it's landing right on top of me. I'm talking that if I ever see you again, I'm going to kill you. I mean it: kill you. Does that about answer your question?"

So who knew?

"Gerry, listen to me. You won't believe this, but I really need your help. First of all, that guy was Russian Mafia. I don't care what the State Department says. Second, just by coincidence, I've got another Russian Mafia goon in my office and he's had a slight accident. It seems that he almost burnt his nuts off and is in no shape to move around. I need him incommunicado for the next two days. Someone's life depends on it. I wouldn't ask if it wasn't important."

I could hear Gerry breathing on the other end of the phone. But that was it. Finally, he spoke. No yelling. It was almost a whisper. "Ian, there's something seriously wrong with you. I mean it. You don't have all of your oars in the water. You need some kind of professional help. You're sick. Are you telling me that you just tortured this poor guy?"

But for the understanding of friends. "Gerry. This poor guy you're talking about is a trained killer. He probably has more blood on his hands than the lead surgeon at Mass. General. I needed information so I got it the best and fastest way I knew how."

"Ian, you're home now. You're not on assignment overseas. You're not in Panama or Nicaragua or wherever the fuck you were. We have laws here. If not U.S. laws then at least the laws of God. And believe it or not, you have to obey them just like everyone else."

I did not want to get into a discussion of philosophy with the man, but I needed his help desperately. "Gerry, can it, will you. I've heard this lecture before. Believe me when I tell you that if you can do this one thing, you will be helping your country in ways you can't even imagine. Not to mention the fact that you'll be saving a life. So how 'bout it?"

Gerry laughed. "You never stop, do you? You never give up. Geez, you'll use anyone to get what you want, won't you?"

He was going to do it. I could tell. "Only my friends, Gerry. I always thought that that was what they were for. To turn to when you're in trouble."

"If you stop the bullshit right now, I'll do it. Otherwise forget it."

I kissed the phone. "You're a prince, Gerry."

That only produced a grunt. "I'm a moron for even listening to you. Okay, here's what's going to happen. I'll put this joker in a hospital under our protection for forty-eight hours. That's it. Two days. After that I'm letting the bastard go. Understand? Letting him go. Just forty-eight hours."

Gerry's word was still golden. A half hour later, two state troopers showed up with the paramedics and took the man with the two toasted marshmallows away.

Before they did, Tommy and I had agreed that Tommy had better make himself invisible before they arrived. I asked him to meet us at the Harbor View apartments in about an hour. In the meantime he decided to pay a quick visit to his uncle to get his wound checked out.

34

After Tommy had split and Gerry's men took the Russian away, I walked out to Kathy, who was still sitting in Mrs. Casey's chair.

I stared into her eyes from across the room and tried to read any hint of a message or outright revulsion.

Kathy suddenly put her hand over her mouth, stood up quickly, and mumbled, "I've got to get away from this smell." Then she ran from my office, through the reception area, and out into the hallway.

I caught up with her just as the down elevator showed up. We rode down to the lobby in silence, ignoring Frank as we walked out the front door and stood together in the warm sunshine that bathed Park Street.

I pointed at an empty bench just across the street in Boston Common. "Why don't we perch ourselves on that for a few minutes?"

She nodded quickly and headed toward the bench before I got the last of the words out of my mouth.

She was already sitting by the time I got to the green wooden bench that looked down a small hill toward the Frog

Pond of Boston Common, which still had a few inner-city kids and some tourists availing themselves of its cool water.

I sat down next to her and watched as she pulled her pack of Newports out of her purse. She pounded the open pack against her left palm and several cigarettes extended from the opening. She next moved the pack up to her mouth, clamped her lips around one, and pulled it out of the pack.

She then produced another Bic lighter out of her right pocket. I had tossed the other one in my trash can when its job had been completed. On the fifth flick, she got it to light. As she brought the flame up toward the tip of the cigarette, her hand was shaking so much I thought she might set her hair on fire.

I reached over, gently took the lighter from her hand, and lit the cigarette. Once it was lit, we sat in a very awkward silence for several minutes.

I broke the silence with a clichéd question. "Do you want to talk about what just happened?"

Her head was tilted down when she shook it and muttered, "Nope."

I inched over toward her. "Do you want to talk about anything?"

"Nope." Again from the same position with the same tone.

I took in and let out a very long breath. "You understand I had to do that. That they are going to kill Barkagan very soon and that was the only way to find him."

"Bullshit!" She screamed it at me so loud that the kids and tourists in the Frog Pond a hundred yards away stopped to see where the scream came from.

Kathy lowered her voice as she looked over at me with

undisguised anger in her eyes. "That's a lie, Ian! You tortured that poor bastard for one reason and one reason only. So you can find out where Ivanchenko is and kill him . . . or die in the process."

I started to object but then she flashed her right hand in front of my face like a stop sign.

"Don't even try. Just do us both a favor and be quiet." She jumped off the bench and started walking up the path that led toward the State House.

I ran up next to her and whispered toward her right ear. "What the hell's with that? You mind telling me where that anger is coming from?"

She stopped and turned to face me. "You can't be as stupid as that question implies."

I tried to answer but she cut me off again.

"Ian, I know you want to get even with Ivanchenko. I know you want to kill him for what he did to your girlfriend and un-born baby. I know that hate now fuels your mind."

She then reached over and took my right hand in hers. "But I also know that was a long time ago. You not only deserve a life, but you have to start living one again. I know you have to let go of your past and try to find a future. Believe me, I know. You have to let it go."

My eyes started to water as I answered with my own raised voice. "Pardon me, but it's my time to say 'Bullshit'!" You and Phil used me like a dull tool to protect your piece of property from harm. You deliberately dangled revenge in front of my eyes, and I all too willingly took the bait. So, as I said back in the office, since when did the Agency decide to get all philo-sophical and spiritual?"

"Go to hell." She spat the words at me and ran up the path.

I sprinted after her and once next to her, tried to match her very quick stride.

"Kathy," I said with my voice still shaking, "I am stupid, but I also do get it. I don't want to even remotely admit how close I feel to you right now. It honestly scares me to think about it."

That got her attention as she came to an abrupt stop in front of the steps that lead from the common up to the gold-domed State House.

She started to say something, and I put my index finger against her lips. "Shhhhh. Let me finish, please. I know that what happened to Irena was a long time ago. I know I owe it to myself to get a life and move on. I know all that."

I shook my head and continued. "The fact is, I think I was doing fairly well in that department until Phil and you presented me with this assignment and . . . nightmare."

"Ian, I—"

Index finger on the lips again. "Shhhh. The Agency had a problem to solve, and I was the perfect tool to use and abuse. Once the desired motivation was agreed upon, the Agency sent Phil and then you to implement its plan. You know what? No problem. I used to work for them and know and understand how they operate. Some people there will ultimately use anybody and, many times, burn anybody to achieve their objectives. I knew that going in."

As I was about to continue, a cloud of smoke from the cigarette Kathy dangled from her right hand wafted into my nose. Why is it that no matter what position a nonsmoker assumes to duck cigarette smoke, the smoke will still find a way to attack him?

I stepped back a couple of feet and continued.

"Okay. So here we are. You and Phil have successfully activated my 'Revenge Sequence.' Congratulations. But guess what? It's not that easy to shut off. Yes, I want to kill Ivanchenko. I want to do so desperately. Believe it or not, not so much because of my lingering hate, but because he really is evil, and, if left unchecked, will inflict more pain, more misery, and more death on countless other people. Some people just need to be exterminated no matter what, and he's one of them."

Now Kathy's eyes started to fill with tears. So much for the two of us being hardened spies.

"I'm sorry, Ian, for what we've done to you. So sorry."

I reached out and took her left hand. "Look. It's okay and I'm okay. I really am. As I said, yes, revenge is on my mind, but I also do want to save that troll Barkagan from the fate worse than death that is about to befall him."

Kathy wiped her now leaking nose with her right hand and looked up at me. "So what do we do now?"

I had actually given this some thought. "Well, the way I see it, we've got a little time to spare before Ivanchenko realizes his errand boy has not come back. So . . ." I smiled.

"So . . ." Kathy smiled back at me. "You were thinking that maybe we could memorialize our friendship."

"More or less. Well, actually more. I was thinking that before we jump back into the shark tank, that maybe we owed ourselves some quiet time."

Kathy's smile grew to a grin. "Okay. Well . . . what's that building at the end of the park?"

"Well, first, the park is called Boston Common."

"Whatever."

"And second, that building would be the Copley Plaza hotel."

"Interesting. And would that particular establishment have 'quiet time' rooms?"

"They do. Five-star, in fact."

Kathy tapped the crystal face of her Burberry watch. "Time's a-wasting. Let's saddle up."

Her grin then graduated to a welcome laugh.

"And I do mean, saddle up, cowboy."

35

Once in our room at the hotel, I knew we had an hour at best. But it was *our* hour. And we were alone. I wanted it to be special for this woman who was becoming so special to me. I wanted it to be right. I wanted to create a memory for the two of us in case the worst should soon befall us.

In this business, you always deal in absolutes. You try to think of every possible thing that could happen in a given situation, and then plan for each one. In this particular case, however, I had to contemplate only one minor detail: the probable imminent death of one or both of us.

As far as we knew, the next hour or so was all we had left on earth. I wanted to make the most of it. I have been accused of being slightly possessive with women. So be it. Right now was the time to be selfish. For both of us to be selfish, caring, crass, and loving.

I have also been accused, all too often, of being a romantic. I admit it. I'm an incurable. I believe in romance. I believe in women. And I believe in the moment.

We sat on the bed in silence. But it was a very comfortable silence. It was a most welcome silence. It was a warm silence. I watched as the sunlight filtering in between the thick blue drapes of the hotel window cast multiple shadows across Kathy's beautiful tanned face. I could see the disk of the sun reflected in her deep brown eyes. Eyes that mesmerized me.

Kathy caught me staring at her and smiled.

"A penny for your thoughts," she said.

It was now or never. "As strange and high-schoolish as this may sound, I think I'm falling in love with you."

She reached across the bed and held my hand. "I know you are, Ian."

That's it? I thought. She knows I am. Nothing else? Since the day we first met, we'd had a very flip, strange, and sometimes adversarial relationship. Knowing that, however, I also believed that along with the sexual tension that seemed to hang between us was an emotional bond that at least I thought was growing with each passing day. I was a hopeless romantic who believed in love at first sight. But apparently I was the only one in the room who thought that way.

"Is that all you have to say?" I asked.

"Yes," she said. "That's all."

"Oh, I guess I understand, then."

She started laughing uncontrollably.

"What's so funny?" I asked.

She wiped the tears from her eyes. "It's your face. It looks like someone just kicked your puppy."

I nodded my head. "Yeah, I guess it does. Well, in a way, maybe someone just did." My voice had taken on a coldness that surprised me.

"Ian?"

"Yes?"

She leaned closer to me on the bed. "I didn't say I was falling in love with you because I'm not."

"Okay. Fine. So you're not. It's no big deal anyway."

She stroked the back of my hand with her fingertips. In spite of my coolness, my heart started beating faster.

"I'm not falling in love with you because I'm already in love with you."

"You are?"

"Yes. As strange as that sounds and as bizarre as you are, that seems to be the case."

I got up from the bed and gently pulled her by the hand into the middle of the room. Once there I pushed the play button on the CD/radio, which, purely by coincidence, was playing Frank Sinatra's greatest hits.

I next walked over to the window and closed the curtains. Now the only illumination we had came from the light in the bathroom. Its muted yellow light fell into the room with just enough strength so as not to make it obtrusive.

"May I have this dance?" I asked as I bowed before her.

She fell into my arms and I melted. This is what love was supposed to be. Only, why did it have to come at such a dangerous time?

As we moved around the room to "Strangers in the Night," I slowly unbuttoned her black vest. Undressing another person while you're slow dancing is tough, but not impossible. I progressed nicely. Standing there looking at Kathy in her bra and white lace bikini panties was almost too much to bear.

I picked her up in my arms and carried her back to the bed.

Our lovemaking that hour was tender. It was wild. It was slow and it was fast. But most of all, it was right. And it was ours. No one would ever be able to take this time away from us. Not even Ivanchenko.

36

The Harbor View apartments were located on Atlantic Avenue, next to the New England Aquarium. They were twin towers of concrete, encasing very small, overpriced apartments. But, if you were a wealthy, Ivy League–educated real estate developer, then money was no object. Location and view were all that were important to you. It gave the stuffed shirt and his wife something to brag about at the next cocktail party they attended.

I wondered if they would also brag about the cockroaches and rats that were rumored to infest the place. Probably not. It would clash with his story on how he swindled some nuns out of the orphanage they ran for crippled blind kids so he could build another shopping mall. The rich, as a contributing segment of society, in my humble opinion, suck.

Comrade Ivanchenko and the boys from the former USSR were holed up on the tenth floor, in apartment 1014. The problem was getting in to see him without an appointment. I mean, it would just violate every standard of good manners. It was so common. So un–Martha Stewart. One simply must have an appointment.

It was the end of the business day in Boston, and that

meant lots of people hanging around the Harbor View apartments. They were sitting on the benches and seawall that bordered the complex as they chatted while enjoying the cool ocean breeze. A female friend of mine and I had shared many a lunch at this very same spot.

It's a very pleasant ambience. You can sit and watch as the planes take off and land from Logan. Or you can watch the sailboats with their colorful sails try to navigate flotsam, jetsam, or the occasional dead body in the bluish-green harbor waters.

Or, if you felt like being an animal philanthropist, you could feed part of your lunch to the seagulls. My female friend Mathilda and I used to feed those guys all the time. It was fun. They would hover over the water, about ten feet in front of our faces. We'd throw them a piece of bread or pizza or whatever. They would catch it in midair, eat it, and then try to crap on our heads.

As Kathy and I walked toward the front doors, I was thrilled to see Tommy standing by the seawall throwing shell-covered peanuts into the water. As he did, I momentarily wondered who or what else he had thrown to the bottom of the harbor over the years.

He'd added a long black trench coat to his ensemble from earlier in the day. Tommy's uncle had apparently fixed him up pretty well. He appeared healthier in the setting sunlight.

Other than nodding, he didn't say a word as he fell in step next to us.

Kathy, Tommy, and I were met by the Harbor View apartments' security team as we walked inside. Two guys in gray blazers walked over to us. The taller of the two seemed to be in charge.

"May we be of service to you, sir?" he said to me as he warily eyed Tommy's immense frame.

I looked over these two "gentlemen." They would be more at home breaking up a strike with baseball bats than they were in this lobby. But hey, we all have jobs to do. Their job was being a gorilla in a suit. Civilization is a nice thing.

They both wore little gold-colored name tags. The taller one's said "Matt."

"Hi, Matt. Yeah, you can help us. We want to visit some friends of ours on the tenth floor."

Matt took a break from looking at Tommy to gaze longingly at Kathy before forcing his eyes back to me. "If you could tell us who your friends are, we'll give them a call and let them know that you're here."

I smiled at Matt and his short but oh-so-wide fellow strikebreaker.

"Well, you see, Matt, that's going to be kind of a problem. We'd really like our visit to be a surprise."

Matt shook his head and crossed his arms across his chest. As he did, I noticed Tommy reach inside his trench coat.

"No way, sir. We have to inform the tenant that they have visitors. It's a rule. Now what's their name?"

Was that a hint of hostility I detected in his voice? Matt was not turning out to be a gracious host. First the aggressive body language of crossing his arms, and now the hard edge to his voice.

I shrugged my shoulders at his question. "Well, that's going to be another problem, Matt. You see, I don't think the name I give you is going to jibe with your records."

He gave me a big smile that showed off his slightly irregular teeth. "Well, why don't you try me anyway."

You just can't reason with some people. "Sure thing, Matt. The name is Ivanchenko. Vladimir Ivanchenko. And he should be in Apartment 1014."

Matt went behind a desk and punched a few numbers into a white Dell PC. Here I was thinking that this guy would have a tough time reading Dick and Jane without moving his lips, and he was using a personal computer. I was almost ashamed of myself.

"You're out of luck, pal. The tenant of record in 1014 is a guy named V. Putin. Sorry about that."

Why did I think that he wasn't sorry at all? "Really, Matt. I'm guessing that current events and world history were not your best subjects in high school. I'm pegging you more as an exceptional shop student. Am I right?"

Matt squinted his eyes at me. "What's that supposed to mean?"

"Nothing worth talking about. Listen, I don't think that Mr. V. Putin is going to be back for a while, Matt. And when he does come back, I think that you can expect his voice to be a few octaves higher."

Matt and his partner didn't say anything. They just stared at us and tried to look tough. Time for a fresh approach.

"Matt," I said, "this young lady works for the United States government, and she feels it is very important that we get into that apartment unannounced."

Matt was not impressed by this new revelation, either. "Oh yeah. Well does she have a warrant? No warrant and you don't get in. It's as simple as that."

Matt was starting to get on my nerves. "A warrant? Sure, I have a warrant, Matt. It's right here in her purse."

Before leaving my car, I had taken my Sig and put it in

Kathy's purse. It was a little too big to conceal under a golf shirt. I pulled it out of her purse and stuck it in Matt's face.

"My warrant is right here, Matt. Does it look official enough for you?"

Matt and his friend had automatically put their hands up. Such was the power of terror.

"You want to go up to 1014, then go right ahead, we won't try to stop you," Matt said with a bit of a stutter.

Tommy chuckled as he swiveled his head back and forth looking for witnesses who might stumble upon the scene.

It was a very magnanimous gesture on Matt's part, but he must have felt I rolled off the turnip truck yesterday. "There's been a slight change in plans, Matt. I would now be very pleased if you and"—I looked at the other guy's name tag—"Rich would be so kind as to accompany us on our journey upstairs."

They both nodded their heads as I herded them toward the elevators. As we rode up to ten, I very quickly explained to them what was going to happen. "When we get outside the apartment door, I want both of you guys to lie down on your stomachs and lace your fingers behind your heads."

I had liberated the apartment passkey from Matt on the way up. He didn't seem to object. My mind was racing a mile a minute. After all these years I was once again about to confront the man who instilled so much hatred in me. A man who had executed Irena as if she were nothing more than a mad dog. A man who did not deserve to draw another breath. A man who epitomized everything wicked about the human race. A man whose time, I hoped, had come.

But what if he wasn't in the apartment? The thought started my heart pounding. But it was just a fleeting thought.

I knew better. I *knew* Ivanchenko was there. He would not let his prize possession out of his sight. With him the mission was all important. Squeeze every million out of Barkagan and then kill him. Simple as that. No gray area.

As sure as I knew Ivanchenko was in there, I was also sure that he was most likely about to kill me. I was beyond over-matched and needed surprise, an element of luck, and divine intervention to survive.

I'd seen Ivanchenko's updated Agency file. Kathy had brought it with her. It had made interesting bedtime reading. Since I had last seen him in that awful, damp, and dark cell in the bowels of Lubyanka prison in Moscow, Ivanchenko had continued to practice and improve upon his craft.

From Afghanistan to Cuba, to Mexico, to Venezuela, to Germany, to Romania, and to the United States, Ivanchenko had escalated his torture and murders. First in the name of the KGB and then when that gig went south, in the name of the Russian Mafia. By last count, the CIA had estimated that he had personally executed over one hundred men, women, and children, including and especially my unborn child. The time had come. Revenge or death was upon me and there was no turning back.

The elevator doors opened at the tenth floor and the five of us walked out and slowly down the hall to 1014. Once outside the door, I had Matt and Rich lie down on the floor as instructed. I made sure they were out of the line of fire, for which they looked eternally grateful. After what was about to happen, they were not going to budge an inch until their mommies showed up to change their diapers.

I put my ear to the door and listened. I could hear the faint sounds of a cable news program coming through the door. I whispered to Kathy, "How are you feeling, kid?"

She attempted a smile, but it didn't quite reach her eyes.

"I feel okay."

"Is that the truth or is that bullshit?"

She held my arm. "It's total bullshit, Ian. I'm scared out of my mind."

"Me too," I said.

I watched as she clicked the safety off on her pistol.

Because of Kathy's looks, one could easily forget that she was a consummate professional in a dangerous business.

Tommy took his Remington shotgun out from under his trench coat.

I took a deep breath and let it out slowly. I couldn't seem to keep the palms of my hands dry. I had to keep wiping them off on my pants leg. I was afraid the Sig was going to slip out of my grip any second now.

I looked down at the woman I was in love with. One whom I was now asking to take a terrible risk. Much the same way as I had done years earlier with Irena. Maybe the shrinks were right, and we do tend to repeat our worst mistakes over and over again.

"Ready?" I asked.

She nodded her head and proceeded to lie on her stomach facing the door with her pistol in front of her ready to fire.

I turned to Tommy. "Ready, bro?"

He took a standing position just to my right with his right foot planted between Kathy's prone legs.

"Let's do this," he said in an unnaturally calm voice.

I slowly eased the passkey into the lock. I just as slowly turned the key and doorknob.

Every time my heart would beat, it sounded like a cannon going off in my ears. Just as I started to open the door, I stopped. They had the chain on the door. Figures. I pointed this out to Kathy, who only shrugged and nodded her head.

She was right. We had come this far. No way could we back out now.

I took two steps backward and threw my whole body weight against the door. The door flew open and I landed on my face in the living room with my weapon bouncing from my damp grasp.

Directly in front of me, one of Ivanchenko's goons jumped up from the sofa he was sitting on and reached under his coat. Tommy stepped forward and blew a hole in his chest before the goon's weapon even cleared its holster.

I caught a glimpse of Ivanchenko running into a back bedroom as his man fell lifeless against the sofa. Just as he was rounding the corner, it looked like one of the three shots Kathy got off hit him in the back.

I ran after him and got there just as he was putting his gun to Barkagan's head.

I leaped and caught Ivanchenko around the waist. It was like hitting a fire hydrant. His gun went off and I heard Barkagan scream. Tough shit, professor. I had more important things to worry about at the moment. Like saving my own life. I had never come up against anyone as strong as this man. Shot or not, it was like trying to wrestle a slab of steel. If he ever got up, I would have no chance. I was a dead man. I moved with an instinct that is ingrained in all of us. An instinct that is barbarian. Animalistic.

As I struggled in a blind panic to retain my position atop one of the planet's most feared killing machines, drool flew from my mouth and speckled the back of his shirt.

As it did, he managed to spin to his side and glare up at me with the instant recognition and certainty that I in fact did not possess the strength needed to keep him down or kill him.

"Your time has come, Ian," he proclaimed in an eerily calm voice. "You are about to join your bitch traitor in eternal rest."

I screamed out with such force that it felt as if my vocal chords had just shredded.

I had been very lucky in one all-important respect. When we had crashed to the floor, we landed between the bed and the wall, with very little room for him to move or defend himself.

I had to act right this second or never get another chance. Ivanchenko would kill me the second he could finish turning his body over. Of that there was no doubt.

Knowing that, I took the risk of half standing. The move and the decreased pressure on his back caught him by surprise. But just for a millisecond. As he started to react, I drove my left knee into the side and back of his left shoulder and kept him pinned to the floor.

It was now or that eternity for me. I quickly laced my fingers in front of his forehead, placed both knees in the middle of his spine, and pulled his head back as hard as I could with a strength I did not know I had.

As I did, I whispered out a scratchy "This is for Irena and my child."

We struggled wildly for about another five seconds before his neck and spine snapped at the same time.

He was dead. I knew he was dead, but I still could not stop myself from pulling his head back even farther. I could hear someone screaming my name over and over again. I finally realized that it was Kathy, as she pulled me away from the now grotesque figure of Ivanchenko.

I lay down on the floor and broke down. The tension had

been too much. The pain all too real. My body jerked from crying spasms. Kathy ran over and sat beside me on the floor. She put my head on her lap and stroked my hair and forehead. All those years of hatred and it was over in less than a minute. It did not seem right. Did not seem fair. Phil had been right. It did not make me feel better. But for all that, I still felt that a score had been settled.

I looked at the horrible sight through my tear-filled eyes, mentally asked for God's forgiveness, then prayed.

Tommy walked quickly into the room, surveyed the damage, and said with a wink, "Good work. I got to split before Johnny Law shows up."

As he turned to leave he stopped and looked down at me while he also nodded in Kathy's direction.

"Oh, and by the way: You were right. She does grow on you."

Several minutes after Tommy left, I found the strength to stand up. Once upright, I found that my knees would not stop shaking from the adrenaline that was being pumped through my body. We walked over and checked Professor Barkagan. He was still alive. It looked like most of his right ear had been blown off, but that was a very small price to pay to be given a second chance at life.

His left wrist had been handcuffed to the bedpost. Someone else would have to free him from that. I didn't have the energy.

I stopped and took one last, long hard look at Ivanchenko. It was a grotesque sight, but I felt absolutely no remorse. His eyes bulged in death. His tongue was sticking out of the corner of his mouth. And there was a small puddle of drool on the carpet next to his head. It was a death I would not have wished upon anybody. And yet it wasn't enough. This was the monster who had killed Irena in cold blood. Who had executed her before my very eyes. The hate once again flared in my mind. I walked over and spit on the carpet next to his lifeless body.

"Hell is too good for you, Ivanchenko."

Kathy held me as we walked back out to the living room, where we were greeted by four of Boston's finest with their weapons drawn and pointed in the general vicinity of our heads.

One of them shouted, "Put your hands up, now!"

I looked at Kathy and then back at him. "Aw, go screw yourself, Jack!"

37

They brought us down to police headquarters and just as quickly released us when Kathy's one phone call had produced a return phone call from the mayor's office. I was glad Kathy had such exalted friends.

"Listen," I said as we walked down the front steps of police headquarters. "I've got all of this Agency money in my bank account now and suddenly nothing much to do, so I was just wondering if you would allow me the honor of spending some of it on you by taking you to Bermuda for a week or two?"

She threw her arms around my neck, kissed me, and hugged my battered body. When she was finished, she stepped back, looked up into my still watery eyes, and said, "Bermuda's great. But you know what they say: It's better in the Bahamas."

I steadied myself on the granite stairs and looked down into her smiling brown eyes. "Is that a promise? I hope that's a promise because I really need a whole lot of better . . . and then some."

ACKNOWLEDGMENTS

First and above all, I would like to thank Anthony Ziccardi for his belief in me and this project. I am truly humbled and honored to be in his stable of authors.

Next, I would like to thank Frank Breeden of the Premiere Authors Literary Agency. Frank is a good friend, an incredibly decent person, and an amazing agent.

Within the Threshold Editions/Simon & Schuster family, special kudos go to Andrea DeWerd for her hard work, patience, and continual support.

I would also like to recognize Kevin Smith for his wise counsel and friendship. While he may like the wrong sports teams, he really does know a thing or two about the English language and plot structure. I own any and all mistakes in the book. Both because I am a moron and stubborn. Usually not a winning combination.

I'd like to thank my father, John MacKinnon, for his early review of the manuscript and his suggestions.

I would like to acknowledge Susan Winstead for her constant encouragement and belief in me.

A loud shout-out goes to Kathleen Connolly for her valued friendship and advice.

Finally, and as always, my deepest gratitude goes to Patrick Ryan Ovide (O-Vee-Dee) for his constant inspiration and love and for being "My Best Friend In The Whole-Wide Universe."